Table of Contents

A New Jersey Christmas Carol

A Special Edition of A New Jersey Christmas Tale

• • • •

With a Commentary on Charles Dickens's A Christmas Carol

• • • •

Paul John Hausleben

• • • •

The cover design and the cover concept by Mr. Paul John Hausleben
The author's photograph and all drawings and artwork are by Mr. Paul John Hausleben
The photograph of Mr. Charles Dickens is from the public domain

"To Old Fezziwig. Please, you have a glorious soul. Go and dance forever. We will cheer you on and tap our toes in rhythm to your steps."
Paul John Hausleben
01 April 2021

A New Jersey Christmas Carol
A Special Edition of A New Jersey Christmas Tale

• • • •

With a Commentary on Charles Dickens's A Christmas Carol

• • • •

Paul John Hausleben

Acknowledgements

Thank you to my friends and family. Thank you to the many readers who wrote to me and conveyed how much they enjoyed *A New Jersey Christmas Tale* and told me how the book is now a part of their own Christmas season celebration. That is very special and dear to me.

Thank you to the readers and associates that planted the seeds as to the origins of the original title versus the alternate title for this special edition! As always, thank you to Mr. Harry M. Rogers Junior. Many thanks to Lydia for her reading, edits, and for the support and feedback. Thank you to Mr. Charles Dickens for writing the greatest story of all stories and for the glorious inspiration.

"Remember, Mr. Steed, it is not what you gained in life but what you sought that counts the most."

. . . .

SINCE JUST ABOUT THE first day after I first published *A New Jersey Christmas Tale,* many readers simply refer to the book as *A New Jersey Christmas Carol.* I have even had my own slips of the tongue and referred to the book by what must be its unofficial alternate title.

I had a dedicated reader, who reads most of my books and materials and frequently contacts me via email circuits, write to me after Christmas in 2023. In the email message, he told me how his family and he all have a new tradition of reading *A New Jersey Christmas Tale* during the Christmas season. They usually begin reading the story about a week or so before Christmas and finish the book on Christmas Eve or on Christmas Day. It was very humbling to hear of this family tradition with one of my books and to hear that I was part of their holiday celebrations; even more so, since I have my own tradition of every Christmas season, of reading my all-time favorite story and book of *A Christmas Carol* by Mr. Dickens.

Then the reader finished off the message with a question.

"One question, Paulie. Why did you not title the book *A New Jersey Christmas Carol*? It seems to be a perfect title for this book, which would make it even more of an instant classic."

Oh, no! Stakes of holly through the heart! Now, the Ghosts of Christmas book titles officially haunted me, from the past, present, and future.

I answered the reader's question with an honest answer.

"Because I liked the way *A New Jersey Christmas Tale* sounded. It had a catchy and retrospective sound to it."

At least in my opinion, it did. Nostalgia at work. It seems as authors, publishers, and editors, do not use the word "tale" too much anymore when referring to stories or books. Since this story reflects a by-gone time and era and alludes to Mr. Dicken's classic story, I liked the word tale in the title.

Shortly thereafter receiving the message from the reader, I spotted an advertisement on the internet for an on-line course offered by a university for enrollment in a course for an in-depth study of *A Christmas Carol* by Charles Dickens.

PJH immediately enrolled in the course. It was back to school time for Paulie. It was a certificate course, but I am not interested in any more degrees at this point in my life. Over the length of the Christmas season, I studied and worked my way through the coursework. The course consisted of about fifteen lectures by the professor via a video, then a wrap up and tests at the end of each lesson. Since I always say that *A Christmas Carol* is not only my favorite book and storyline and the greatest book and story of all-time, I felt as if I knew the book inside and out and upside down and right side and left side up. The university course was the highlight of my 2023 Christmas season. I completed it in a short time with a score of one-hundred percent. It was more than enjoyable; it was wonderful, and the course taught PJH aspects of the characters, and the story, and about Mr. Dickens that I not only never knew, but there were some angles that I never even considered.

Fast forward in time.

In June 2024, while on a creative and writing lull and bent on improving my organization, I was poking and clicking through some notes and files, when I found the notes, the coursework text for *A Christmas Carol,* and the examinations from the university course. Those items combined with remembering the message from the reader and the waves of title controversy over the title of *A New Jersey Christmas Tale.* And to add to the formula and the birth of this special edition book, while organizing files, I found in the PJH writing vault, a commentary on the Dickens masterpiece that I wrote about the time that I was envisioning and writing the outline for *A New Jersey Christmas Tale.*

I intended to publish the commentary piece, along with some Christmas related lists of fun material, in the blog sections on the God Bless the Keg Publishing LLC website. For some unknown reasons, I never published the commentary piece or any of the lists. I put them in the PJH vault and completely forgot about them. Until now!

Ah ha! The picture became clearer. I could use my new knowledge from the university course, fit it into the commentary and expand upon the scope of that commentary to the point that it would enhance not only the experience of reading *A New Jersey Christmas Tale* but also *A Christmas Carol*. The light bulb of ideas burned brightly! A special edition, or should it be a re-titled release? I had never done anything such as re-titling a book before. Was it even possible?

PJH jumped into research of the subject, and yes, I found it done quite often, particularly when a certain aspect of the book or creation becomes very popular. More so than the original author or creator ever imagined. One example came from the music world and one of my favorite musical artists. The late, great Gordon Lightfoot originally released an LP album in the 1970s, and when one cut on the album became a huge hit, the record company re-released the album under the title of the hit single.

At that time, I was unsure of what exactly what I wanted to do with this new idea for a project. Therefore, I set the project aside for approximately three months to focus on and finish other projects.

When I revisited this book, I decided to compose a special edition with the new title and still reference the original title, and include the commentary and some new tidbits such as this section of author's notes and some of my not-so-world-famous lists. The lists are of various Christmas related items, including some ratings about *A Christmas Carol*. Followers and readers of PJH sure know how Paulie loves to make lists and ratings!

This special edition turned out rather well; however, I still feel as if the original title has a special ring to it! Upon close examination of the titles and the stories behind them, I think they can both coexist with each other on their own sides of the bookshelf. Bookends and companions in the literary world of Paul John Hausleben alongside his writing hero. A nice place to be.

This was a fun and enjoyable project to work on and publish. On behalf of PJH, Mr. Dickens, Mr. Steed, Mr. Shook, Old Fezziwig, Ebeneezer, Tiny Tim, and all the others, I truly hope that this work and the original versions all become an enjoyable part of your Christmas season and a part of your holiday celebrations for many years to come.

Thank you for reading it.

Paul John Hausleben

15 September 2024

Author Notes
(From the original edition)

• • • •

THE ENTIRE YEAR OF 2020 was as if it was part of the principal theme for a storyline of a bizarre science fiction novel. The pandemic of COVID-19 brought havoc and upheaval to the entire world. The topsy-turvy reports from an endless stream of experts left everyone in the general population twisting and turning at the horror of the situation. No one knew what to make of the constant changing of the facts, at a gasping media clutching at the prospect of unparalleled ratings, at the horror of harsh rules imposed on a (until now) free society and the destruction of businesses and livelihoods. Then we had to deal with the contrast between the ominous predictions of the end of the entire world to the "oh it is not so bad" type of testimonies. No one could separate the fact from the fiction.

By the time that the holiday season rolled around, everyone was weary of it all and longed for normalcy and some semblance of order in the grand celebrations of the gathering of families, and the joy and peace that the holidays bring to our lives and hearts. It was to be a welcome relief. Alas, it was not to be! More dire straits, more rules and confinements and the lockdowns and madness continued. Everyone made the best of it; including Paul John Hausleben.

I am usually a solitary creature, and this all seemed somewhat familiar to me. I am usually alone at Christmastime; the holiday has long since lost any luster in my own personal life. In fact, I am alone most of the time, so off I went into the PJH Writing Command Center to take the edge off reality with some intense creativity and to be alone with my characters. Christmas was a safe haven for me to write within; having published many Christmas stories already and because of the harshness and bleakness, I found that this particular year it was even easier to dive into the holly, the music, and the inspiration.

And, oh, yes, did I find inspiration!

A Christmas Carol by Mr. Charles Dickens is my favorite story. I believe it is the greatest story ever written with the most colorful and amazing characters of all time, too. Dickens has no peers; in my opinion, he is the greatest author of all time.

Traditionally, every year at Christmastime, most often on Christmas Eve, I sit down next to my Christmas tree with my favorite beverage in hand and I read *A Christmas Carol*. Every time that I read it, I manage to capture something else out of the story that I previously missed. Christmas 2020 was no different because I noticed how the profound genius of the story and its amazing author was actually in the early redemption of Scrooge within the pacing of the storyline. When Ebenezer Scrooge views the Christmas Eve party scene at the workplace where he was apprenticed at as a young man, and absorbs the immense joy and overwhelming generosity of Old Fezziwig, Scrooge is actually a changed man. The rest of the story and experiences simply reinforce his change. Old Fezziwig might be the greatest of all of Dickens's characters and that is saying something special!

When I finished the annual reading of the story, an idea to honor my favorite author as well as my favorite story and my home city and state popped into my head. The fact that *A Christmas Carol* is now in the listed titles in the public domain made my decision easier.

I decided that I would write my own version of the story, not to duplicate it or copy it (as if I could even do that!) but to honor it. I would create my own characters, use the basic premise of good overcoming meanness and sadness and despair, within the magic of Christmastime, and make the setting in my home city of Paterson, New Jersey, in the mid-1970s. Additionally, it seemed fitting to write such a story and help overcome the despair that COVID-19 wrought onto our lives and the holiday season.

Off I went, writing my own Christmas story, and while some basic themes are familiar, there are major and minor changes to the storyline along with an entire cast of original PJH characters. The story flowed easily from the start to the finish. While riding an intense wave of creativity, I wrote this book in seven days.

I hope that by sharing my little meandering of words here within my own memories of the holiday that it invokes some of your own memories and returns you to a time when life was kinder, gentler, and simpler. I also hope that it helps you to realize the magnitude of the genius of Mr. Dickens and of his original story.

Dear reader, I hope that it returns you to a time when if one Christmas light in the string went out; then they all went out, and it began a painstaking troubleshooting mission to find the malicious culprit in the string. To a time when we hung tinsel straight upon the tree branches and took the time to make sure that we did so. Ah, the slightest breeze from the nearby heater, or the slightest miscue, caused the fragile tinsel to loop over the other branches! Straighten them with care now.

I wish to return you, dear reader, to a simple time, before technology captivated us, and to a certain extent ruined us, as it combined with the dreaded social media as it controlled us and guided our every move and thought. To a time when we actually spoke around the kitchen table, and on the front stoop, and to when we read newspapers and spoke on the telephone and did not text or message each other instead. When we sent Christmas cards as seasonal greetings and we listened to the radio as much as we watched television. When journalists were journalists and not activists, when sports were about sports and not about political actions, when we told stories, when we shared thoughts, not constant malice, and discontent. That, dear reader, is my wish for you.

Perhaps it is more of a dream than it is a wish. I hope that I succeed in some small way.

Thank you, Mr. Dickens for writing the greatest story ever written, thank you for allowing me to jump in here with you, and most of all, please, to all the readers, accept my heartfelt thankfulness for reading, and in theory, enjoying my efforts. Thank you for you.

27 December 2020

Mr. Paul John Hausleben

· · · ·

A NEW JERSEY CHRISTMAS Tale honors my old home city of Paterson, New Jersey, and the outlying areas. In honor to Mr. Dickens, where I could do so, I did my best in writing this manuscript to abandon typical New Jersey slang and wording and harken back to how Mr. Dickens wrote the original wording and phrasing with just a touch of "Old English" tendencies. Obviously, it is not typical of New Jersey in the 1970s, nor is it how I usually write authentic New Jersey "speak" in my past work, but I felt as if it was the proper manner with which to compose the work.

27 December 2020

Prologue

It is an easy contraption to assemble. At first, it comes out of the box as a flat and unusually shaped thing. As I hold it in my hand and realize that I need to shape it and adjust it in order for it to resemble a Christmas tree, I go to work. What used to take many hours now only will take me a few minutes, but then again, it is a much smaller tree than what we used to put up in our home. The lights are plug and play L.E.D. types with no more worry about when one light goes out, they all go out sort of thing. The lights all light up handsomely and economically, too.

I place a few ornaments on the tree. A few homemade ornaments from past years, the hockey goalie, a few New York Yankees replica ornaments. There you go . . . the Mick takes his place on a lower branch. I put the battery-powered Christmas train around the tree's base. It does not have the character that the old Lionel train had, nor does it possess the carbon smell from the electric motor brushes, but it works fine enough. Percy Faith guides me along with background music, and within an hour or so, the tree glows with enticing Christmas captivation. I sit in the chair in front of the tree, turn the lights off in my apartment, and admire my handiwork. Admittedly, it looks beautiful.

Christmas is so different this year, and the loneliness creeps into my soul and envelopes me. I have a sudden thought. Dickens! Yes! Scrooge and Marley and the Ghosts, and Bob and Tiny Tim, and of course, Old Fezziwig. They will keep me company. I put away the Christmas boxes that held the lights, the ornaments, and the Christmas tree. Then, after doing so, I dig around in a box in my closet and find the book. After pouring three fingers of Irish whiskey neat into a glass, I settle into my chair and open the blessed book.

I will leave the music on as a backdrop to my reading.

Let me see; now, oh yes, someone is as dead as a doornail. No doubt that he is. He is, indeed!

Here we go now, off into another glorious Christmas season.

Christmas, glorious, Christmas.

Open hearted and slightly tipsy, I wander wide-eyed just as if I was a youngster into all the magic that it brings.

After reading the blessed book. I close the covers and think. I have an idea. A variation on the original theme. Yes! Thank you, Mr. Dickens. Here we go now.

1974.

In the old neighborhood. A mean, old, nasty guy. I have known a few in my time. An old lace factory. A by-gone era.

I can write this. Yes, I can.

A New Jersey Christmas Tale
Chapter One
Mr. Absalom Wickham Steed

IT WAS A DULL, DARK day before Christmas in 1974. Indeed, it was Christmas Eve.

It was a bitterly cold December day, and the cold infiltrated every nook and cranny of life in the good old city of Paterson, New Jersey. Many were mindful of the cold, while others were not. Some people bundled up with heavy coats, scarves, wool hats, boots, and gloves in order to fight it, while others felt no ill effects of the cold. A light jacket and a cap would suffice to ward off the cold. For some people of this good world and a few other worlds both known and unknown, bitterness came built-into their souls. Bitterness was just as if it was another molar or incisor in their mouths.

It bit just the same as those sharp teeth did.

Bitterness was for them, just as laughter is for the joyous. Bitterness came easily; it was a way of life; ingrained, commonplace. If these bitter people were to laugh or smile, no one would recognize them.

On this bitter cold Christmas Eve, the sky occasionally spit out some reluctant snowflakes and the clouds crept lower and grew darker as the day edged slightly past noontime. The weather prediction was for a white Christmas, with the snowfall increasing and falling steadier after sunset.

The prospect of a white Christmas caused a great deal of merriment and joy in the yearly celebration because of the wonderment and the quiet hush it would bring to the season. Snow at this time of year was special. Very special, and even in an old and tired city such as old Paterson was, it covered everything in a sparkle of beauty and white. A refreshing of an aged world.

Today, many were joyous, but a few were not. One person in particular was quite sour indeed.

The old Haledon number fourteen bus chugged along Belmont Avenue as it headed toward the corner of West Broadway and Belmont Avenue. The bus teemed with merriment and joy. Shoppers sat seat-to-seat and arm-to-arm while heading to downtown Paterson, New Jersey to pick up last-minute gifts at Jacobs-29 department store, Meyer Brothers department store, and Stern Brothers and many others. Downtown Paterson was the place to be today!

The hot roasted peanuts at the Planter's Store smelled like Heaven! Lunch at the Woolworth's counter was neck-to-neck and four persons deep in line.

As the old number fourteen bus cruised past Cliff Street and Belmont Avenue, the passengers broke out in a random rendition of the Christmas song, "God rest Ye Merry Gentlemen. . .."

Just around the corner on Cliff Street, a few hundred feet or so of where the bus just cruised by, sat the Steed Lace Factory. The bricks of the foundation and the building's exterior were first placed home in and around 1900, the wooden floors were a set a year later, and the slate roof received a seal coat with a heavy sealing pitch once since then. Roof leaks were just a nuisance in old factories. Buckets worked quite well for the runoff. The factory was old, tired, tarnished, and it stood there on Cliff Street for what seemed as if it was forever, and then some too. Inside the old factory, the lace machines spun loud songs of entanglement as the lace flew off the machines and onto the spinning and eager capture spools. Down in the bowels of the building, the factory's maintenance man, Billy Van Der Sluis, puffed on a cigar, sipped coffee, and watched the old steam boiler as it chugged out heat and power. The giant smokestack that loomed a hundred feet in the air next to the factory puffed out giant exhales of combustion to prove the boiler was in high fire. Wintry days did not welcome low fire on old boilers.

Factory workers on the day shift anxiously scanned their machines, manipulated controls and levers, and continually glanced at their watches for quitting time. Four in the afternoon could not come quick enough! A day off was on the horizon. Christmas Day! Christmas, glorious, joyous, and blessed

Christmas! A blessed and rare day off with full pay! A rarity indeed when you worked at the Steed Lace Factory.

In a drafty old office on a loft, overlooking the main production floor of the factory, stood one of those aforementioned bitter people. His incisors were sharp and his molars were like razors. He had a hardened heart; his bitterness knew no depths, and his smile was long since lost. The last time he smiled, he was nineteen-years of age and he vowed that was the last time. To date, his word was solid and his vow intact. He stood near the partition between the office space and the factory, with his hands behind his back. His keen and beady eyes scanned the factory production floor through the glass for a worker or machine operator goofing off while on duty. Perhaps he will capture a lace cutter snipping off a precious inch or two more of a lace reel than warranted and cause waste and excessive loss, or his eyes might catch a floor sweeper leaning on his broom, or other important aspects of non-production! When you are the owner of the Steed Lace Factory, everything was about production, numbers, and money. Besides, it would give his bitter heart a little touch of glee to terminate a worker's employment on Christmas Eve! Reduce the salaries and wages on the books! No paid day off for that worker! No wasted wages for foolish holidays! Yes, he focused his beady eyes closer, his heart wishing to catch just one worker slacking off!

The bitter man leaned his ear toward the glass overlooking the factory floor and turned his head to listen to the noises down below from where he stood. A particular noise magically loomed above the loud hum and roar of the continually spinning machines. The keen hearing of Mr. Absalom Wickham Steed could pick any errant noises out of the loud and convoluted fray of the clamor of the machines. He had spent a lifetime in his family's factory. He grew up here, matured here, some might even say he died here, but dear reader, if you are to believe and understand this story, then that is the one question best left for the last words!

The owner of the Steed Lace Factory, Mr. Absalom Wickham Steed, was forty-one-years old. He looked as if he was ninety-years old. His long nose was pointy, his chin was pointy and the top of his head, even covered with thin, wispy, and tussled layers of salt and pepper hair, was pointy, too. His long fingers had long fingernails, and they were pointy too. Steed preferred them, untrimmed and pointy. Everything about Absalom Steed was pointy and sharp-edged. He dressed in black pants, a black buttoned-up shirt, and pointy black shoes. His attire accurately portrayed the blackness that surrounded him. This bitter cold Christmas Eve felt like July to his icy heart. He felt no cold, no winds, no drafts, and most of all, he felt no joy. Christmas or otherwise. He wore no sweater or vest even inside the drafty old factory on a wintry day. Steed thrived in the cold and any day that provided a cold temperature inside the factory was his great love and his joy, too. Cold was his favorite medium with which to weave layers of despair and tribulation into his life and the lives of others. He was tall, lean, and mean. Meanness and bitterness emitted from the pores of his skin as sweat did from the skin of a long-distance runner, and it surrounded him with a black cloud of meanness and bitterness that constantly hovered over his head and body and followed his every movement.

Steed bent over at the waist a little and walked in a powerful, purposeful stomping-type of walk. His walk and the tilt to his back were not because of any illness, or injury, or age-related stiffness; it was to crush the world below his feet in order to eradicate any lesser items or something in his path. People that worked with Steed, or knew of him and observed him (people only associated with Mr. Steed only out of absolute necessity; it was never by chance or for the pleasure of daily interaction. He had no friends or associates and no family that he lingered with) often said that his walk was to look for errant coins and the bendiness of his back was from counting his money while bent over his desk. There might have been a great deal of validity to their observations!

Steed's eyes narrowed as he studied the production floor below him through the glass. He leaned his ear against the glass to confirm a noise he heard and drummed his fingers on the glass as he listened.

Steed turned and intently stared at his assistant sitting at his desk in the far corner of the office.

"Shook! What is that infernal noise emitting from the production floor? Shook, come over here. Now!" Absalom Wickham Steed asked and commanded as he screamed at Mr. Wesley John Shook.

"Yes, of course, Mr. Steed," Wesley Shook said as he dropped his pencil into his bookwork and slid his chair out and made his way to the glass window. Mr. Wesley Shook was the manager in charge of production, purchasing, and general services for the Steed Lace Factory. The perception was that Wesley

Shook was Steed's right-hand man of sorts, although Mr. Shook would deny that part of the relationship.

After quitting time on a Friday afternoon, at Hank's Tavern on Belmont Avenue, while sharing a few pints, Mr. Shook would tell his drinking buddies the truth.

"Please, let me set the record straight. Mr. Steed allows no one to become close to him, and furthermore, he allows no one, including myself, to make any important or vital decisions on my own or their own. He is always and completely in charge. Mr. Steed would never allow the perception that he required help or advice of any kind."

Shook's testimony was accurate. Steed was a solitary and bitter human being, not inclined to general human interaction not related to work and business, and for that, all those around him thanked the Lord in Heaven every single day. Steed was not prone to any frivolity or purposes that could not, or did not, earn him money. Frivolity equals cost in Steed's world, and that equation did not work for Absalom Wickham Steed. Anything that impeded work in Steed's world, he saw as unnecessary. He only took time to eat and spent money on food because he required it for sustenance.

Steed looked upon fellow human beings and virtually everything else in the world as simply a vehicle or an item to manipulate and use to earn him even more wealth. Please, dear reader, know that his wealth was mountainous! Piles and piles of money earned over the many years since Steed's grandfather, Mr. Gerald Lambert Steed, began the family business and joined the coattails of the famous "Silk City" of Paterson, New Jersey. There in Paterson, Steed laces and products gained a reputation for the best quality laces in the country and perhaps, even in the world. People proclaimed that Absalom Wickham Steed still had his first earned nickel in his pocket and his first dime, quarter, silver dollar piece, and one-hundred-dollar bill, and in fact, maybe his first million dollars were in a vault in that drafty old house on Preakness Avenue on the outskirts of the city that he lived in. Maybe! Yet, it was never enough wealth. It never is with a man such as Absalom Wickham Steed. Never. Enough.

Mr. Wesley John Shook worked for Absalom Steed for sixteen years, and how he endured that long was a mystery to the world. It was a testimony to his faith and fortitude. His long tenure at the Steed Lace Factory was a validation to Mr. Shook's amazing virtue of incredible patience, his kindness, and the fact that jobs in these old cities were difficult to find. Yet, there was little doubt that Wesley Shook might be a candidate for sainthood. Or so Mrs. Shook said.

When Wesley Shook's time on Earth finally ends, he will meet Saint Peter at the Pearly Gates of Heaven, the good saint will glance at his notes and say, "I see here, Mr. Shook that you worked with that wretched Absalom Wickham Steed for a lifetime. Please, go right in, good man. Go right in."

Mr. Wesley John Shook was a pale white in skin color, paler and whiter than snow. He was short, nearly as round as he was tall, and he was frumpy, round-faced and his kind and wide smile, despite working very closely on a daily basis with Mr. Steed, never left his face. It went edge-to-edge of his full-moon-like head and his thick and generous red hair layered the top of his head like melting ice cream creeps down the edges of the cone. His nose was round and wide, his blue eyes round and wide, and they flickered with a perpetual kindness. His belly was round and wide, his ears, well, they were round and wide too. In summary, Mr. Wesley Shook was round and wide.

Wesley quickly walked over to the glass, stood next to Steed, and listened as best he could through the glass for the infernal noise of which Steed complained and begged for identification. It was difficult to hear anything on the other side of the glass from the production area and above the noise and clamor of the lace machines spinning, twisting, and producing their endless spools of lace. Wesley tilted his head and placed his ear on the glass and he felt Steed's eyes burning a hole through his soul with impatience at a lack of an immediate response from Mr. Wesley Shook.

"Well, Mr. Shook! Is there some type of sudden ailment that arose with you to cause a defect to your hearing?"

"Not that I am aware of Mr. Steed. I just have to admit that all I hear are the usual machine noises."

Steed placed his hands upon his hips, narrowed his eyes, and glared at Wesley Shook.

Steed's voice came out of his mouth laced with angry notes, "Let me assist you to overcome your inadequacies with your ability to hear. There is some music playing down there, Mr. Shook. Music, from what I would guess to be an illicit and unauthorized radio. Explanation! Mr. Shook! Now!"

Steed's anger rose and his voice reverberated above even the hum of the machines.

Shook leaned in and nodded his head while saying, "Oh yes, I do hear it clearly now. God Rest Ye Merry Gentlemen is playing. A lovely rendition by Percy Faith. I recognize the arrangement and orchestra. I am quite the fan of Christmas music."

"Shooooookkkkkk!"

Mr. Wesley Shook trembled at the sound of Steed's voice and he retreated from the glass and took one or two steps back from where Mr. Absalom Steed stood.

The timid and mild-mannered man anxiously and nervously folded his hands together and then rubbed them tighter to gain warmth and some type of courage, too. It was nearly as cold in the office as it was outside today, and now; it grew even colder with the frigidness of Steed's soul penetrating what little warmth there was remaining in the air.

"Yes, Mr. Steed, there is ah, ah, ah, a radio playing in the far corner of the primary production area. The shop steward came to me this morning and asked if they could have a radio to tune into the annual Christmas program on the local radio station WPAT. Every year, they have a program called the Spirit of Christmas. The station plays continuous Christmas music from noon today until midnight tomorrow on Christmas Day."

Wesley Shook finished speaking. He swallowed hard as Mr. Steed listened to his testimony. He swallowed again when Mr. Steed simply glared at him and added no words to the conversation.

Mr. Shook felt the need to enhance upon his initial explanation, and to do so, Mr. Shook spoke with great hesitation in his voice.

"The program plays continuous Christmas music with no commercial interruptions. I mean, the station donates the airtime. It is quite generous of the radio station's management. There are some sponsor announcements at the top of each hour from local businesses for some additional promotion opportunities. Limited announcements."

Another hard swallow.

Steed waved in the air and pointed toward Shook's desk to show that Wesley Shook should return to his desk. Shook gladly turned on his heels and made his way there in order to gain some welcome distance between the two men. Mr. Shook's roly-poly body flopped and bopped as he hustled back to his work post. Mr. Steed watched as Wesley returned to his desk. When Wesley sat down in his chair, Steed turned his back to the office and to Mr. Shook, and Mr. Steed stared out the glass, and observed the production area. Absalom Steed folded his arms behind his back in a letter V shape and clasped his hands together to hold the position.

Mr. Absalom Steed continued to stare out the glass window. He rocked back and forth on his heels and as a prelude to speaking; he cleared his throat and then coughed a little. His words came out of his mouth as if he was spitting pebbles along with the words.

"You are quite the fan of infernal Christmas music, huh, Shook? How nice. Just to confirm your statement, Mr. Shook. A radio is playing Christmas music broadcasted from a local radio station in my production area. Is that correct, Shook? Is that what is the source of the infernal noise? Infernal Christmas and useless merriment."

Wesley Shook stood up from his chair in a vain effort to gain some volume and authority in his voice.

Instead, he answered in a voice filled with apprehension; nonetheless, he answered, "Ah, yes. That is correct, Mr. Steed."

Steed nodded his head, turned on his heels to face Mr. Shook, and glared at Wesley while folding his arms across his chest.

"Is a radio allowed in the production space?"

"Generally, not."

"Generally? When did I ever authorize a radio? When did I ever use the word generally when authorizing something? It is either allowed or disallowed. Generally, Mr. Shook?"

"Yes, Mr. Steed, you never use the word generally. That was my word."

"Interesting, Mr. Shook. Once more, I ask you, did I ever authorize the use of radios, or other frivolity in the workplace? Especially, so a radio! Was it when the production crew asked to listen to the World Series? Or the big football game? Or perhaps when the president spoke?"

"No sir, Mr. Steed. We do not authorize the use of radios in the workplace. However, it is Christmas Eve, sir, and I thought it would be a nice gesture to keep the crew's spirit up. I feel as if a happy team full of cheer and Christmas spirit will be a productive team." Mr. Shook cleared his throat of nervousness, his right leg wobbled a little and after regaining his steadiness, he continued, "If the team is happy then they will work hard and enjoy the workplace."

Steed glared at Wesley shook and shook his head in disagreement.

"You are wrong, as usual, Shook. A comfortable employee, by the way, they are employees not a team, Shook, is a lazy employee. They fall into complacency and become comfortable and unproductive." Steed clenched his fist in a show of grasp and power and then continued his ranting, "You need to make them uncomfortable, always on edge, fearful of losing their jobs, walking on eggshells. That promotes hard work. No handholding and delicate strolls in the park! We have no need for cheer or Christmas spirit here, Mr. Shook."

"Yes, Mr. Steed. My sincere apologies for the miscue. I became lost in Christmas wonder, too."

Mr. Steed folded his arms and then unfolded his arms and walked over next to Wesley Shook's desk and continued to glare daggers at his key manager.

Mr. Steed's ears twitched and his pulse pounded in his temples as he began a long and passionate speech, while Wesley Shook endured every painful word of Steed's long and tedious rant.

"Christmas? Oh yes, silly, silly Christmas. The biggest waste of effort and money in all the year. A ridiculous excuse for merry-making based upon some fable of a virgin birth and a bright star in the sky and wise kings and trumpet blowing angels. The only thing sillier than the notion of wise kings traveling miles upon miles across deserts to bring gifts to a baby is the notion of peace on Earth and goodwill toward men. Keep their spirits up? A team? What are we, a professional baseball team? That is the trouble with you, Shook. You are a cupcake. A softie. You think everything is sunshine and rainbows. My grandfather thought the same things. He was a softie, too. Always being kind, thoughtful, and pleasant to the workers. Working with the labor union to give the worker's hefty wage increases, more benefits, more holidays, and other pandering to the workers and crews. Giving away hard-earned Steed money to charities and to build hospitals. It almost ruined us. Thank goodness, my father, the great, Ryerson Gingert Steed, saved our beloved business when my grandfather retired by stepping in and changing the culture and mindset and returning us to the important business of turning a profit! Ryerson Steed stood tall and stomped all over foolishness of the takers of society. The so-called needy, which in reality are simply lazy and inept fools. My father extinguished the useless donations to charities and hospitals that my grandfather erroneously performed. He closed down the wasteful Steed Foundation that gave away more wealth and rewarded lazy, useless persons, looking to sponge money from our hard work while they sit around and fiddle-faddle their lives away! My father restored the name of Steed to power in this old city!"

Steed quickly turned and pointed at the only piece of artwork or décor in the entire office. It was a faded black-and-white photograph of Absalom Wickham Steed's father. The dreaded Mr. Ryerson Gingert Steed. Despite the words of praise and honor from the son, this was a low budget and unimpressive honor bestowed upon the father. A faded black-and-white photograph that had seen better days. The picture frame appeared as if it was from a five and dime store.

Wesley Shook swallowed hard as he stared at the grimace on the face of the man in the faded photograph, his thin beady eyes staring out in abhorrence at Wesley Shook. There was not a single note of happiness on the face of the man in the photograph.

Wesley never met the elder Mr. Steed, but he heard of his reputation from some of the older workers that remained from that era of the Steed Lace Factory. Ryerson Steed made his son seem as pleasant as a walk in the park on a warm spring day compared with Ryerson Steed's vile nature. Mr. Ryerson Steed's reputation remained; hanging as if it were dark clouds of blackness hovering over everything that had the Steed name emblazoned on it. The elder Steed stomped through life and he taught his son to stomp through life, too. Stomp out happiness, stomp out joy and smiles and compassion and anything that was good and kind in the world. From all testimonies, even to this day; years after he left this world, Ryerson Steed was a forceful, unfair, miserly, harsh, evil, cunning, conniving, and covetous man.

Steed turned back and faced Wesley Shook once more.

"Shook, why do we not allow radios and frivolity in the workplace?" Steed quizzed his manager on one of his many rules for perceived success.

Answering with the answer and statement that he had heard a million times before, Wesley chirped up the words as if he was a parrot on repeat, "Because it is an unnecessary distraction that leads to poor production and to the promotion of foolish errors because of a lack of focus on work and productivity."

Mr. Steed clapped his hands together so loudly that Wesley Shook jumped up from his chair.

"Correct! Did I not reward the union with a generous wage increase this past year? An entire nickel added to their wages under intense pressure from the evil business managers, whose only mission is to shake down honest business owners to squeeze and grab more and more profit out of our coffers for less and less work. Let me tell you, Shook, that my father was correct and these unions will eventually kill American business with their unfair demands for more and more with less and less work and production! Did I not agree to give them Christmas Day and other preposterous holidays off from work with full pay? Did I not agree to the late shift's request to leave early with full pay when the clock strikes midnight tonight for silly Christmas? Is that not generous enough?"

Wesley swallowed hard once more. It was becoming a habit now.

"Very generous, Mr. Steed."

Steed seemed satisfied with Shook's agreement. He sat back on his heels, and his ears twitched upon hearing the words.

"Did I not give you a generous wage increase of a nickel an hour a few years ago, Shook?"

"Oh yes, very generous of you, Mr. Steed. Eight years ago, when I found that error on the shipping manifest that shorted us materials and netted us a refund of almost ten thousand dollars."

Steed peered in with his beady eyes, as his mind seemed to ponder the news that it was eight years ago since Mr. Shook last had a pay increase. His ears twitched again.

"Have you found anything else since then to net my company ten thousand dollars because of errors of the aforementioned lazy fools of this world, Shook?"

"No, sir."

"Well, then, do you think you deserve to pick my pockets for more money for no tangible results?"

"No, Mr. Steed. I am very . . . happy here."

Steed strolled back to the glass, rocked on his heels again and once again placed his arms behind his back as he did before while gazing out at his production floor. He clasped his hands together behind his back, studied the production floor with his beady eyes and pointed features.

Steed spit the words out of his mouth in a growl.

"Then, I assume you would not want to spend your beloved Christmas holiday while standing on the unemployment line."

"No, Mr. Steed. I apologize for my error."

"Why did you allow it?"

"Because it is. . .."

Steed interrupted with loud words and cut-off the words of Wesley Shook.

"I know! I know! It is Christmas! Well, Mr. Shook, if you want to retain your position here at the Steed Lace Factory, then I strongly suggest that you hustle down there and confiscate that radio and never let me see or hear of a radio in the workplace again! If the radio is the now soon-to-be former property of one of the workers, then he will forfeit it for bringing prohibited contraband on my property. Let him file a grievance that I will gladly rip up in his face."

Wesley Shook nodded his head, jumped from his chair, and bolted in the direction of the office door.

"Mr. Shoooooook!"

Wesley Shook's spine shivered as he hit his brakes hard just as he was about to leave the office.

Steed waggled his long, pointy index finger in the air toward Mr. Shook as more words, pebbles, and stones spit out of the edges of his mouth.

"As a side note about business. Not that you will ever be much of a business manager because of your feeble mind, your softie nature and cupcake stature. However, as a side note and a gift of lending some of my great business knowledge to you, let me tell you of the foolishness in a radio station canceling business and revenue for such a stupid thing as broadcasting Christmas music without commercials. Ha! Not to mention the sheer stupidity of the sponsors spending good money to have their company name and mission mentioned only once during an entire radio broadcast. How ridiculous. For the average consumer, they only hear the silly music. Unless they drill it into their stupid heads by constant repeats, they will never recall the sponsor's efforts or names, or nature of their business."

Mr. Steed screwed his already twisted face up into an even tighter turn of the screw than it ordinarily was; while the pain of pondering some sort of business offered for free or lower than market value worked at his soul.

Mr. Steed continued his protest and to state his position.

"Instead of canceling commercials," Steed said while he walked to his desk, pulled out the chair and sat in it while glaring at Wesley, "they should triple the price or even charge more for the air time! If stupid people want to enjoy Christmas music for their absurd celebrations, then charge them for it! Supply and demand! You want happy, merry Christmas music. Then you must pay for it! More Christmas waste and drivel. Silly business moves! Ridiculous! Never give away anything for free that the public needs or demands! Profits, Mr. Shook! Profits. Now, go get that wretched radio!"

"Yes, Mr. Steed. Thank you for your wisdom and profound business advice."

Steed grunted, nodded, and Mr. Shook disappeared. When the door closed, Steed stood up from his desk. He walked back over to the window and watched as Wesley Shook wobbled across the floor. Mr. Shook shut off the radio and unplugged it from the electrical outlet as the workers howled in protest and waved their hands in the direction of the window where Absalom Wickham Steed watched in delight. Steed rubbed his hands together in satisfaction that another piece of unnecessary frivolity met its demise. Steed was about to turn away and return to his desk when he watched one of the floor leaders and workers, Mr. Jonathan Shaw, cross the floor and waved his hands rather violently at Wesley Shook. A brief conversation ensued, and even through the glass, Steed could easily determine that the protest was over the confiscation of the radio.

Steed rubbed at the crown of his head while pondering and mumbling, "Ah, very good. That cupcake Mr. Shook is in a bad spot now. He deserves it for being such a wishy-washy dishrag. His plump little legs quiver when he is nervous. Such a softie he is! It must be Shaw's radio."

Steed's delight at the uncomfortable scene bubbled over, and he narrowed his beady eyes more while he scanned the worker's faces and their hurling of protests at the confiscation of the radio. Steed also noticed a small table on the production floor; it was a table near to where the radio sat. A table that stood gloriously full of some boxes of chocolate, some fruit, and some other assorted food and snacks. Some of the boxes were open, the workers were enjoying the candy and fruit, and there were remnants of Christmas wrapping paper and ribbons around the boxes. Some boxes were unopened and remained intact.

Absalom Wickham Steed spoke aloud to the walls of the office. Steed lived alone in a solitary existence and speaking aloud to himself or to the walls was commonplace in his life.

"Ah, ha. Hallo there. What is this? I surmise they are holiday season gifts from vendors. Snacks and food and candy and fruit. More unauthorized contraband on the production floor. More infernal Christmas celebrations! More bending of the rules by Mr. Shook."

Steed's eyes continued to scan the production floor, looking for more items astray and procedural violations of his rules. He noticed something much more disturbing than some Christmas gifts. An idle machine!

"And why is Shaw not on machine number thirty-eight? That is our best performing and our highest production machine."

Steed's beady eyes scanned machine number thirty-eight and Steed quickly determined that it sat idle and unused today. Steed continued to study the scene below his viewing window.

Mr. Shook kept the radio tucked under his arm; he shook his head and pointed toward machine number thirty-six. Shaw protested a little more and then gave up and strolled back to machine number thirty-six to resume his work.

Steed mumbled, "I better check the latest production numbers from the report that Shook placed on my desk last night. It is readily apparent that if I don't watch every aspect of this business, everything slips into the cracks!"

Now concerned about his beloved production, Mr. Steed quickly made his way to his desk to find the report and study the numbers.

The door to the office opened and Wesley Shook squeezed his portly frame through the door, and, still with the radio tucked under his arm, quickly made his way to his desk.

"Shooook!" Steed looked up from his paperwork, yelled and waved at Shook. "Bring the contraband here."

"Yes, Mr. Steed."

Wesley walked over and gently set the radio upon Mr. Steed's desk.

"I do not recall commanding you to place the contraband on my desk, Mr. Shook. Did I not say to bring it here, Mr. Shook, rather than set it upon my desk? I dare say your hearing is defective. Set it there on the floor next to the file cabinet."

"Yes, Mr. Steed," Shook said as he picked the radio up and set it in the requested spot.

"I see that it is Shaw's radio."

At first, upon hearing the words, Wesley Shook seemed slightly surprised at Steed correctly identifying the radio's owner, until he realized that Absalom Steed must have watched the event and interaction through his viewing window.

"Yes, it is, Mr. Steed. Correct."

Steed still looked down at his papers, with his pencil in hand, while circling figures on a ledger sheet.

"Shook, please tell me why it is that, Shaw, one of our most productive operators, is not on our best performing machine. Which machine is that, Shook?"

Wesley Shook did not hesitate in his answer, because despite Steed's belittling and unrelenting downplaying of Wesley Shook's abilities, Shook was quite capable, and, in fact, excelled at his job. He knew his work.

"That would be machine number thirty-eight. That machine is down for service. It has some motor issues. I am waiting for a service call from Worrall's Machinery. Until then, I moved Mr. Shaw over to number thirty-six," Wesley Shook explained the reason for the move and stood next to Mr. Steed's desk and studied his face.

Steed's ears twitched at the words. He placed his pencil down in the ledger and leaned back in his chair. Then after reconsidering his work, he placed the pencil in such a way as to mark the exact location that he worked on in the ledger.

His eyes then turned to Mr. Shook and Steed asked, "When did the machine go off line, Shook?"

"Last Friday afternoon, around four in the afternoon. I had Billy Van Der Sluis look at it, but he said it was a major issue, so I called Worrall Machinery."

"Last Friday and today is what day, Shook?"

"It is Tuesday, Mr. Steed."

Mr. Steed nodded and his eyes burned holes into Wesley Shook.

"Why then, is Thomas Worrall not here with an army of men, repairing my most productive and lucrative machine? Does his service agreement not state immediate service for emergencies at no extra charge, with service provided twenty-four-hours a day, three-hundred, and sixty-fix days a year and seven days a week?"

Once more, Wesley Shook's hard swallows came in large gulps.

"It does, but his top mechanic is off for . . . ah, ah, off for, Christmas (Wesley hesitated to even mention Christmas) and Tom's wife has been in the hospital with chronic kidney disease. A transplant seems out of reach at this point. She is not doing well at all. The disease is advanced. He asked if he could be here on Thursday. The day after Christmas when his daughter was off from work and she could stay with his wife and attend to her needs."

Steed's pointy ears twitched with the words. He folded his pointy fingers and hands in his lap and spit more words and pebbles out of his mouth.

"And what part of that story is my problem, Shook?"

"Sir, well, I guess that it is, of course, not your problem."

Mr. Shook's legs quivered in nervousness while he ventured into even more dangerous waters by interjecting some of his facts into the conversation, "We have forty-one other machines on-line. Mr. Steed, as of an hour ago, our production schedules are far ahead of projections in light of the upcoming holidays. We will actually ship product ahead of time."

"Mr. Shook, it is your job to make sure our production crew produces superior lace products and that the Steed Lace Factory ships that product ahead of time or right on schedule and my expectations are for those tasks to happen efficiently and productively. If you fail my expectations, you will lose your position and I will replace you with a more effective production manager. The facts remain. I have a production machine down and I should not have to remind you that we are in the production business, Mr. Shook. I am bleeding money here. Loss of production. Loss of earnings and profit. Wasted space and square footage on my production floor with an inoperable lace machine. Worrall's service contract obligates him to the terms and conditions, and he did not deliver on said terms and conditions. A service agreement that I might add, costs me a fortune for reliable and trustworthy service. Service that Worrall chose not to deliver."

Steed picked up his pencil, twirled it in his fingers for a second, and then suddenly slammed it down upon the desk so hard that poor Wesley Shook jumped out of his shoes. Wesley Shook blinked several times and you could see the pain upon his face at enduring the twisted logic lecture of "Steed-facts" from Absalom Steed.

Wesley Shook finally spoke and tried to enter some justification for his position, "Well, sir, I understand, but Mr. Worrall did say he would be here bright and early on the day after Christmas, sir. He has always provided superior service and high-quality repairs and maintenance in the past."

"Shooook! Correct! In the past. Not now. Mr. Worrall will not be on site here until the day after Christmas! When his service agreement clearly states immediate service. Yet here we are, five days later, and the machine remains inoperable. You and your cupcake demeanor allowed it! It does not mention infernal Christmas as an excuse in the service agreement, or sick wives, or mechanics off from work while happily dancing around Christmas trees. Service, Mr. Shook! Service upon the agreed terms."

Steed stood up, then leaned in over his desk with both hands, palms down on the top of the desk, while bracing his long, lean frame as he stared at Wesley Shook.

"Now, place your softie ways aside, and call in Tompkin's Machinery. Tell them you will award them the complete service agreement if they can get here today and repair that machine. Get here today at a reduced service rate per hour. Do it, Mr. Shook! Tompkins has been after the business for a long time and he will agree to the reduced rate to get the business."

"Yes, Mr. Steed."

Steed slowly sat down in his chair and added, "And Shook, immediately terminate the service contract with Worrall."

"But Mr. Steed, Mr. Worrall's wife, is very ill. It has been a huge financial burden on him. He has been with us for fifteen years and it will mean the loss of his most lucrative service agreement. Mr. Worrall might lose his business."

Wesley's Shook's kindness overpowered his fear.

Steed narrowed his eyes even more in a fire glare at Wesley Shook. A glare that could melt paint off walls and curl your toes and make your spine shiver.

"Once more, Mr. Shook, I think you need to see a doctor for a check on your hearing. Or, perhaps, I need to find a replacement manager, with improved hearing abilities. Since you are wasting my valuable time repeating myself, why not waste some more of it with another repeat of my previous statement? Once more, what part of Mr. Worrall's situation is my problem? Mr. Worrall chose to make poor business management decisions. He chose to give his mechanic off from work for infernal Christmas. He chose to marry a woman who became ill. His choices, not mine. People get sick all the time, Mr. Shook. They live, they get sick, and they die. Extension of sympathies on my part does not put profit in my ledgers, or any wealth in my bank accounts. Terminate. The. Agreement. Now."

"Yes, of course, I will, sir. To restate my thought process, I just thought because of the circumstances and the long-term business relationship, and of course, after all, it is. . .."

Wesley John Shook felt the burn, and he cut the words off before he once more mentioned the hated Christmas holiday.

"Yes, Mr. Steed. Right away, sir."

"Another thing, Mr. Shook. I noticed a table down there on the production floor. A table full of candy, snacks, fruit baskets and chocolate and such. It appeared as if the workers were enjoying them."

"Yes, Mr. Steed. There is a table down there on the production floor. They are gifts from vendors and contractors, and I shared it with the production teams. I thought it would be a pleasant gesture for . . . Christmas."

"Ah, yes, a pleasant gesture for infernal Christmas, Mr. Shook. Very nice of you, indeed. Mr. Shook, is food, shall we use your previously chosen word of, *gen-er-ally* allowed in the production area?" Absalom Steed chose a high-pitched voice to speak the words in a purposeful mocking of Wesley Shook.

"No, sir."

"As are not radios."

"That is correct, Mr. Steed."

"Well then, this just gets worse and worse for your management choices, Mr. Shook. It is so exceedingly pleasant of you to share gifts with the workers. Especially, pleasant, when it is my money that pays for the service contracts and vendors. Therefore," Steed said as he crossed his arms upon his chest, his ears twitched and his beady eyes narrowed to tiny slits as his gaze turned into a burn directed at Wesley Shook, "those are my gifts. I suggest you hustle down there, gather them all up, and place them in my automobile. Remove the infernal Christmas wrapping paper and silly ribbons and bows. I, unlike you, Mr. Shook, want nothing to do with any part of infernal Christmas."

"Yes, Mr. Steed. Right away," Wesley Shook nodded and quickly spun on his heels to confiscate the gifts when Steed called out to him and caused Wesley to pause in his mission.

"And Mr. Shook, if you value your position and do not want to stand in a merry Christmas unemployment line, while having all the time in the world to listen to your beloved Christmas music and identify every tune, then my strongest advice to you right now is don't touch that thermostat on the wall there by your desk. I saw you fiddle with it earlier today and now that snow is on the way and the weather is turning colder as the day wanes, I see you eyeing it again now. I instructed Van Der Sluis to push all the steam to the machines. Heat, Mr. Shook, and warmth, is overrated. Furthermore, in deep repentance over your many errors and mistakes and in acknowledgement of my generously paying you an entire day of salary for zero work on infernal Christmas Day, make sure you are here at the crack of dawn on Thursday. The very crack of dawn."

Chapter Two
Christmas Eve Visitors

ABSALOM WICKHAM STEED stayed at work, in his office, until well past seven o'clock at night. The snow became heavier and steadier after five o'clock, but Steed had little regard for weather. He felt as if he lost too much time this afternoon with as he continually mumbled, "Infernal Christmas" and the ensuing related discussions with his perceived bumbling manager, Wesley Shook. Tompkin's Machinery had instantly responded to the service call, even late in the afternoon on Christmas Eve to repair the broken machine, as it was obvious, they were very eager to put on a display of great service and then receive a lucrative preventative maintenance and repair service agreement. The second shift would go off line at midnight to celebrate Christmas. Steed could not bear the thought of losing a day of production to infernal Christmas, therefore once Tompkin's Machinery's mechanics left and Wesley Shook left for the evening (he dared not to whisper any merry Christmas greetings within earshot of Mr. Steed) then Absalom Steed decided it was time to pack up his books and head home. He could just as well pour over and examine his numbers there as he could here, and he did not have to deal with the pain of watching the second shift leave early. After carefully packing his briefcase with his ledger books and paperwork, Steed noticed the radio on the floor next to his desk near the file cabinet. Right where Wesley Shook had set it. For a reason, unbeknownst even to Absalom Steed, he bent down, picked up the radio and tucked it under his arm. Out the door he went, shutting down lights to preserve precious electricity along the way. Into the snow, Steed went; bent over in a perpetual scowl while stomping on the snowflakes as he plowed toward his car parked in the lot.

IT WAS A DULL, DARK house. Immense, threatening, and ominous; looming like a black cloud that an artist painted into the side of the hills of the edges of the Preakness Mountains overlooking Preakness Ave in Paterson, New Jersey.

Preakness Avenue twisted and turned and climbed and fought with the same edges of those mountains as it made its way out of the old city. The avenue was a major travel route from the edges of the Hillcrest and Totowa sections of the city to touch the borders of Wayne Township, and the roadway led the way into the more bucolic areas of Wayne Valley. Preakness Avenue was a path to escape the clutches of the urban outpost of the old Silk City. On a snowy Christmas Eve, with a few inches of snow on the roadway, the steep inclines made for a precarious ride for a vehicle navigating the hill. Vehicles slipped and lost speed and spun tires, and gripped and clawed their way up the hill. Some drivers gave up and turned around and would try the long route around the mountain to make it into Wayne Valley. The plows of the city's road maintenance crews were on the way, and the salt and sand thrown earlier were wearing out in the effort to provide traction. Most vehicles crawled.

Most, but not the vehicle driven by Mr. Absalom Wickham Steed. His vehicle plowed right through the greasy snow on the roadway as he made his way toward the dark, dull house nestled into the edges of the hills of the Preakness Mountains. Snow and ice stood no chance against his vehicle and his bitterness. His bitterness pervaded right through the weather and melted the ice and snow under his tires. Nothing stood in his way or even wanted to cross paths with Steed. Even something as formidable as cold and ice and snow proved to be.

Steed drove a 1966 black four-door sedan equipped with a V-8 engine, solid steel bumpers, a pointy interior to match the exterior and interior of the pointy owner and a portentous presence. It was even a little more foreboding than a hearse was. The car had been Steed's father's car, and it was old and bitter, just like Steed was. It was the perfect vehicle to transport bitterness and meanness in while riding hither and dither. Absalom Steed never bought new items; he held onto the old items and possessions that he had forever and then some more time.

The vehicle weighed a ton already, but it had deep-treaded snow tires on the rear with strap chains that Billy Van Der Sluis installed earlier this afternoon, along with a few bags of sand that he dropped in the trunk for added weight.

Steed plowed up Preakness Avenue, hunched over the pointy steering wheel with his pointy face and his beady eyes peering down his pointy nose while frowning and chastising the vehicles all around him that could not navigate the treacherous snow-covered hill.

Steed mumbled aloud to the pointy interior while watching a low-hung sports car in front of him lose traction and momentum on the hill and slow to a tire-spinning crawl, "Fools! Idiots! Too stupid to watch or listen to weather forecasts and prepare your vehicles for proper transportation to your employment and obligations in inclement weather. Wasting money on fancy sports cars that are worthless in the snow and depreciate to mere pennies on the investment six months after purchase! The fool driver is most likely heading to church or some other infernal Christmas celebration!"

The downhill lane of Preakness Avenue was clear of cars, so Steed swung his giant tank-like vehicle around the sports car, plowed onward and he sounded his horn while shaking his fist at the helpless driver of the slipping sports car.

"Stay home, fool!" Steed screamed while hunching over the steering wheel even more. He plowed up the road, snow dancing from his snow tires, the snow chains clanking and singing with success on each rotation of the tires hitting the roadway underneath them. He made a right turn just before the road hit the border of Wayne Township and then made the first right-hand turn into a driveway for the Steed's estate. A long, long, winding path that led to the dark, dull house at the top of the driveway. The driveway was steep and fresh snow covered the entire length of the drive. Steed hit the gas pedal, and the vehicle laughed at the virgin snow. Up the hill he went, he pulled the car in front of the home and parked it underneath the large portico next to the home. Steed grabbed his lunch pail, his briefcase containing his ledgers, notes and banking account information and other important papers (these were a constant presence in his life) and in a few seconds, he exited the car. With a flip of the key, Steed locked the doors of the car, while focusing his beady eyes into the falling snow and darkness. He looked around in the snow for any fresh footprints that might signal an ambush and stomped and plowed his way up the long porch and to the front door. He walked hard, as if he could eradicate the snow and ice and anything else in his way with his steps. Steed set the objects on the porch floor and then stomped back to the vehicle to get the radio and the gifts that Wesley Shook placed in his car. Within a few trips, Absalom Steed had unloaded the car and placed everything on the porch floor.

Steed equipped the front door (as well as all the exterior doors in the home) with four locks, although the door itself was sufficient protection for a castle or fortress of old. The door was solid oak, no viewing windows for intruders to break, and the finest local craft workers constructed the door in and around 1920 or thereabouts. A person would require a substantial ramrod combined with superior muscles in order to break it down. Steed pulled his collection of keys from his pocket, operated all the locks, swung the door open and stepped inside the home. He stuck his pointy face outside the edge of the door, narrowed his eyes into the snow to make a last check of the landscape, and now satisfied there were no intruders nearby, Steed gathered the objects and his belongings from the porch floor. Within a few trips, he had everything set inside of his home on a nearby table in the huge entrance foyer. The only piece of furniture in the foyer. Steed slammed the door shut and redid the locks, and the echoes of the slamming door reverberated throughout the old mansion. He also slid the four-deadbolt sliders across the door edges too, and secured the door tightly into the old wooden frame.

In its heyday, the home was a showplace of prestige. It was always immense, but not always threatening. In fact, the home, at one time, thrived with love, joy, and care. It was a sprawling home with ten bedrooms, an exclusive master suite with a vast bedroom, private sitting and study quarters, and an adjacent expansive bathroom. Additionally, there were five other full bathrooms spread out amongst the mansion, and some powder and sitting rooms. The first floor also possessed a showpiece of master craftsmanship, with a towering center staircase trimmed in coveted chestnut wood trims, graced by a large entrance foyer with dual hanging glass chandeliers.

In an era of long-ago, the entrance foyer of the home, at this festive time of year, boasted a towering Christmas tree, fully decorated to the hilt. However, this Christmas Eve, there was no Christmas tree there in the foyer; instead, there was only some lonely dust. On the expansive first floor of the mansion, there was a library with chestnut bookshelves, a dining room, and a sitting parlor, along with a maid's quarters and a gourmet kitchen.

Many years ago, the grounds and the property surrounding the mansion were elegant, with garden sheds and other outbuildings, and flower gardens and shrubs and a neatly manicured landscape set between majestic trees. Gerald Lambert Steed built the estate with the early profits of his exploding business of lace, and while he was proud of the home, he was most proud of the location of it. He often told the story of scouting out the perfect location for the home within the nook of the Preakness Mountains, and he would proudly show visitors the breathtaking display of the city of Paterson from his library windows. Mr. Steed purposely built the home so that his library windows took in the view.

Gerald Lambert Steed married and raised his two children here. The Steed family consisted of one girl and one boy, born three years apart. Marilynn Dorothy Steed was the oldest and Ryerson Gingert Steed was the younger of the two siblings. Ryerson Steed married and raised his only son here. Absalom Wickham Steed grew up in the home, and to this day, he still never left. Now, he was alone in the home and in his life.

Gone now were the flower gardens, and the garden shed roof caved in and the outbuildings fell into disrepair. The shrubs were overgrown, and the trees hid the property as they towered even taller than some edges of the surrounding hills did. Maintenance was expensive, and elegance was frivolous.

Steed removed all the artwork from the library walls and the rest of the walls of the home. No art, no flower vases, no family photographs, no decorations of any sort. Just cold, stark bareness and cobwebs and dust. He removed all the books from the library's chestnut shelves. There were no servants, no maids, no cooks in the kitchen, no landscapers or gardeners, no other persons were in or around the home these days. There was no elegance left here at all these days; only a dull, dark, cold, dusty home. Absalom Steed did not mind dust. It fit into his life, as did the darkness and the cold and the drafts and the emptiness. None of those cost money or required any investments of any sort. Therefore, it all worked well for Absalom Steed.

He closed off all the bedrooms and bathrooms except for the smallest of the rooms, which he used for his own quarters. He closed off the library and the parlor and any other space deemed unnecessary or frivolous. No need to heat unused square footage! Steed removed most of the furniture, only keeping what he required for the bare minimum of life. A few chairs, his bed, a dresser for his clothes and some folding tables. In the kitchen, there were just a few pots and pans, a handful of silverware, some bowls and a small cooktop and a small refrigerator. The larger appliances were idle and unused.

Absalom Wickham Steed spent Christmas Eve sitting at an inexpensive folding table set alone within the confines of an otherwise barren dining room, pouring over his precious general ledger filled with numbers. Endless numbers, twisting and turning over and over, while churning in his mind within an endless circle of greed. Because enough money is never enough money. Besides, you never know when you might find a decimal point in the wrong location that tilts the ledger even more in your direction! He nibbled on some of the fruit and crackers from the gift baskets that he confiscated from the factory workers and heated a small container of soup; he poured it into a chipped coffee mug and sipped at the soup while he worked. Steed required very little nourishment; in theory, his massive wealth kept his heart beating and sustained him.

When the clock struck eleven o'clock and only one hour remained for this Christmas Eve, Absalom Steed folded up his ledger, set aside his pencil, and he turned off the single light bulb on the old dusty lamp that, in theory, illuminated his work. Steed set the boiler thermostat control dial down to fifty-eight degrees because heat was frivolous, expensive, and unnecessary and then he rinsed his mug out and crept off for his bedroom. On the way to his bedroom, his beady eyes spotted the radio that he took home. Steed had set it on the folding table when he entered the home. Similarly, as before this, Steed had no reason as to why he had an unexplained attraction to the radio; he admittedly despised all forms of entertainment. He did not own a television, or a radio, nor did he own a record player or care to listen to music or even listen to the local news broadcast. Steed occasionally read the newspaper for headlines, the stock market reports, and the weather and tossed the rest aside. Yet, for some reason, the radio beckoned to him. In a repeat of the same mysterious reasoning of why he picked it up and brought it home from the office; he reached over to the table where he had set it, picked it up, tucked it under his arm and carried it up the stairs to his bedroom.

The bedroom was as sparse as his heart and soul were. Steed only had one lamp in the entire room and he did not turn it on, preferring to navigate the darkness by familiarity. He loved darkness and thrived within its inky blackness, mostly because it was free but also because it kept his soul dark, too. He turned the three deadbolt thumb latches on the bedroom door and slid the heavy deadbolt across the top. The entire set of locks gracefully slid into place with resounding mechanical clicks that afforded Steed some sense of security in their proposes.

Once inside the bedroom, Steed placed the radio on the table next to his bed. He felt along the wall, peered into what little light he had in the room, and found the electrical outlet on the wall. Without any fear of an errant finger into the electrical outlet, Steed plugged the radio into the electrical outlet. Even electrons dared not to infiltrate or associate with Mr. Absalom Steed! Steed stood next to the table and stared at it for a few seconds, pondering exactly why he did so. He still felt it was strange for him to consider listening to the radio; but after a few seconds of thought, Steed shook off the wandering of his mind and moved onto another mission. A very important mission!

After setting the radio in place, Steed crept over to the wall behind his bed, and used his knee to move aside his bed frame. He tapped carefully on a strategic location on the wall to reveal a hidden panel, and then opened the panel while peering around in the darkness of his bedroom. He required reassurance that he was alone in his bedroom. After all, there might be someone or something else there with him in the inky darkness who might spy on him. The panel revealed a hidden wall safe and, after looking around once more, Steed reached down to his neck and tugged at the lanyard that hung around it. A lanyard equipped with a key dangling from the end. He took the key, felt along the front of the safe for the keyhole, slipped the key in the lock and spun the safe open. He carefully tucked away the money clip from his pocket, a few spare coins, and then snapped the safe door shut, removed the key from the keyhole, rehung the lanyard around his neck, and hid the safe once more. Absalom Steed cackled in delight with his love of his hidden wall safe. He enjoyed very little, if anything, in life, but he enjoyed hoarding and protecting money. Even if it was merely pocket change and some extra dollar bills.

After using the bathroom to wash up, Steed changed into his bedclothes, donned his winter robe, and stomped off to his bedroom. He rechecked the security of his bedroom door, then scanned the darkness for anything out of place and carefully tilted his ears for errant noises. After a careful recheck, Steed took off his robe, hung it on the bedpost and he climbed into bed. He laid there in the bed, with his hands folded across his body, and he stared at the ceiling. For some reason, Steed's soul remained disturbed and uneasy.

The house was silent, cold, and quiet.

Outside the sprawling home of Absalom Wickham Steed, and the surrounding expansive grounds, while echoing down the valleys of the Preakness Mountains, the snow peacefully drifted down on a silent world that prepared for the arrival of the blessed Christmas morning.

On this most blessed night of nights, magic happens. In so many ways.

Steed rolled over in his bed and stared at the radio. The tuning dial glowed in the darkness; even though the radio had no power. The lure was too powerful, too magnetic; too unknown and after giving up what little resistance that remained, Absalom Steed, reached over, turned the power button to the "ON" position and clicked the radio to life.

Immediately, after springing to life, and while the tuning dial just barely illuminated, the radio's speaker blared the music out, "God rest ye merry gentleman, let nothing you dismay. . .."

The glorious melody of the familiar tune filled every nook and cranny of the dusty bedroom; in fact, it filled every nook, cranny, and corner of the dusty, dark, dull old home.

"Huh? That is strange. The radio has vacuum tubes. It should've had a long warmup time. Instead, it came to life right away. It must be a new-fangled, hybrid radio with instant on. Ridiculous," Steed mumbled as he peered in suspiciously at the radio.

"Let nothing you dismay," once again, the words echoed in every part of the home.

Somewhere deep in the depths of the home, inside the plaster walls, in the depths of the basement near the boiler, in the rafters of the attic, somewhere, the words took root and hope came alive where it previously was lost and wayward.

"Infernal Christmas music! It is a curse upon humanity!" Steed cried out while reaching for the tuning dial in a desperate attempt to tune off the radio station that was being so bold as to broadcast such annoying drivel on Christmas Eve.

"What has gotten into me? Why would I even do this? I should have never turned this blasted radio on," Steed said while his fingers frantically spun the tuning dial in an effort to shut off the infernal Christmas music and broadcast of joy. Yet; Steed did not reach for the power button, only the tuning dial.

He stopped tuning when the speaker blared with another radio station, "God rest ye merry gentleman, let nothing you dismay. . .."

"Infernal Christmas is a plague! It's everywhere tonight. Is there no news going on in the world? Or has Christmas cancelled everything else out?" Steed complained aloud as he turned the dial knob once more, only to discover the same music, and the same tune playing on the radio from the next radio station on the dial. Steed spun the dial once more and landed upon the next radio station on the adjoining frequency on the dial. The same identical tune blared out of the radio's speaker! No matter where the tuning dial landed, the radio played the same music, the same verse, the same stanza, the same tune, the same musical artist.

"The tuning dial and system must be defective! No matter where I tune, the radio remains stuck on this one station!" Steed cried out into the darkness.

Suddenly, the words of his manager, Mr. Wesley John Shook deeply resonated from the depths of his memories.

"Oh yes, I hear it now. God Rest Ye Merry Gentlemen is playing. A lovely rendition by Percy Faith. I recognize the arrangement and orchestra. I am quite the fan of Christmas music."

The words of Mr. Shook were loud and clear in his mind. Furthermore, to compound his present amazement and confusion, Absalom Steed recognized the tune, the arrangement, and the music. It was the same version of the song that played this afternoon in the production area of his factory and it was the same tune that Mr. Shook identified earlier today in the afternoon.

At one time, Absalom Wickham Steed enjoyed music. He, in fact, he was quite the music aficionado. At one time, Absalom Steed enjoyed life and the many aspects of it. At one time.

Not now, not on this blessed Christmas Eve, but at one time.

Frustrated and dumbfounded, Absalom Steed flipped the power button on the radio to the "OFF" position; he forcibly tapped the top of the radio with his hand and rolled back into bed, and he tightly pulled the covers up to his chin in an effort to shut out the entire world and this disturbing event. The dial lamps no longer glowed and the blessed song faded away into the inky darkness.

Steed allowed his eyes to wander around the room. He was alone. Very alone.

Steed welcomed the quiet. The undisturbed dust.

"Infernal Christmas is an incessant plague!" Steed bellowed as he sat up in bed and he allowed his eyes to wander around the room one more time, before pulling the covers up to his chin, and flipping over onto his side to try to go to sleep.

Midnight arrived and Christmas Eve gave way to Christmas Day. Christmas, glorious, Christmas. Midnight Christmas masses and other church worship services were now over, the hymns of praise sung, the greetings exchanged, and Christendom returned home to await the good news and the joy of Christmas.

Down below the Steed mansion, on the other end of Chamberlain Avenue, the bell in the bell tower on Saint Gerard's Church on West Broadway pealed and welcomed the magic of Christmas. The church tower bell at Cedar Cliff United Methodist over on Zabriskie Street in Haledon Borough joined in the celebration, as did the bell at Saint Mary's Episcopal Church, and over on Haledon Avenue in Prospect Park Borough, Saint Paul's Church joined in the midnight chorus. An ecumenical chorus welcoming in the sacred day and celebration. The joy of the chorus of the bells echoed throughout the night and made their way through the snowflakes all the way to the ears of Absalom Steed. He lay in his bed, wide-awake and listened to the chorus.

The joyful pealing of the bells, of course, annoyed Mr. Steed.

"Why must those wretched church bells sound at midnight to announce ridiculous Christmas? There ought to be a law against such noise pollution. Waking people at midnight all across the city and the boroughs for stupid Christmas nonsense!"

Steed once more pulled the covers up to his chin and he was rolling over on his side, when he heard the pealing of the bells slowly fade away into the night.

Then, a new noise arrived after the pealing of the distant bells finally died away.

Old homes make many strange noises. Especially so at night. Late at night.

Often, it is the frame of the home settling down, even so many years long after construction, other times, it is the blowing off of the dust of the ages, or sometimes, and it can be a harkening to the past and an awakening to the future.

The noise started low, almost as if it was a signal of air bound pipes from the boiler far down below Steed's bedroom. In the bowels of the home. It happens sometimes; expansion and contraction, the boiler is in high fire, then low fire, a valve somewhere in the line, has some loose packing. Then there are warm days and cold days and the air infiltrates into the loose packing, and eventually, the air pushes to the highest parts of the system. It causes a thump-thump in the radiators and pipes. Steed had heard it many times before this time. It was a bitter cold night tonight, but last week it had been a little on the warm side. For late December in northern New Jersey, that is.

Steed was sure of the cause of the noise while he carefully listened to it with the covers still pulled up tightly around him. It was a thumping from deep within the depths of his home.

"That wretched boiler! First, those horrible church bells and now, a clunky boiler! Can't a man get any sleep around here? I will need to get Billy over here to bleed the air out of the pipes," Steed spoke to only the walls.

On the other hand, was it only the walls?

"Thump, thump, thump, thump."

First, it seemed as if it was a noise in the pipes, then it was on the staircase, and then it resonated outside his bedroom door in the hallway. It echoed all around and Steed sat up in bed with the covers still pulled up around him, while carefully listening. His eyes darted around the bedroom and for a fleeting moment, he even debated turning on the radio to drown out the noise! No, no, no, this noise was not the pipes, or the boiler. It was something else. Something ominous, something or someone had bypassed the deadbolts and the locks and the solid oak door. Yes! There was something or someone in his home. Something unknown.

If only for a moment, for the first time in forever, Steed regretted his incessant and persistent thriftiness.

Thoughts raced in his mind, 'An intruder must have broken in, despite my cautiousness and improved security.' His eyes darted to the safe well hidden behind a faux section of wall in his room, where only he knew of the location.

He was sure that his money was safe. 'If only I had a telephone installed in this room,' he thought, 'I could call the police on this intruder.'

"Thump, thump, thump, thump."

Steed pulled the bedcovers off as the sound grew closer and louder, and then he slowly stood up. His mind whirled with possibilities, wandering from intruders, to noises, from snow and falling icicles on the roof, to air bound heating pipes, to the possibility that he was dreaming and sleep walking; however, one thought above all made his skin crawl in a million heebie-jeebies. The noise sounded just like the noise that his father's walking cane made when he navigated the staircase. A walking cane that his father used late in his life to assist him in his walking and daily navigation.

His father's actions and his memories remained vivid in his mind, even if he had been dead for almost eleven years.

"Nonsense! I must be feverish!" Steed cried out while touching his forehead and then his neck and chest to test his body's temperature.

"I heard Shook sneeze today! I bet he gave me some type of germs and I am coming down with illness! I need a weapon. Something for defense," Steed said as his eyes searched through the darkness for an object to use in order to ward off the intruder and to defend his home. Suddenly, the radio turned on, the music loudly returned, and Steed turned while horrified at the illuminated dial and gasped as the radio once more blared out, the same tune, "God rest ye merry gentlemen, let nothing you dismay. Remember Christ our Savior was born on Christmas Day. . .."

While making its joyful proclamation in song, the radio's dial lights cast a low light upon the entire bedroom.

"Wwwwwhat is happening?" Steed stuttered the words as he now moved quickly in the radio's direction to switch it off or unplug it from the wall. However, he stopped in his tracks and watched in horror as the deadbolts on his bedroom door slowly turned and the deadbolt latch moved open under its own power or by an unseen hand or power!

Steed heard the mechanical sounds that the locks made, and now, he dropped to his knees in horror as he watched while the door slowly opened. Absalom Wickham Steed fell to his knees while trembling at the scene unfolding in front of his eyes. He had no power to flee, no strength to look for a weapon to defend himself with; his body shook in great waves of fear as his mouth hung open and his eyes opened wide. He no longer was cocky or brash or bold and his usual attitude of bitterness gave way to fear. He looked small now, rather than the larger than life, abusive man known to berate the world with verbal insults and curse every person living within it with his presence. Within a few quick minutes, his fear made Steed seem small, meek, and irrelevant.

While the music played on endlessly in the background from the radio, Steed's beady eyes narrowed even more than usual and he carefully watched in horror as, within the now open door, what appeared to be a flame slowly appeared before his eyes. It was, at first, tiny, and it flickered and danced before his eyes. The flame hovered a few feet from the floor, and then it grew brighter and stronger and slowly took shape. The flames licked the edges of a rough outline of a human form. The flames worked outward from the bright center with the edges of the flames slowly drawing and shaping the outline before Steed's eyes, as it slowly took the shape of a human being. Specifically, a man. While the flames slowly lessened in intensity, Steed slowly stood up to try to stand on his feet. His trembling legs made that a wobbly adventure. He held onto the bed frame to steady his body. When he stood up, the flame burst into a bright light that was so brilliant that Steed had to shield his eyes from the glare. When the glare died away, there in front of him stood an outline of a transparent man. The figure had no visible skeleton, no bowels or a heart or lungs or any inners. It was just an outline of a human form, almost as if it was detail white pencil drawing of a human being on a black paper background. Steed could see through the figure while it stood there; in fact, he could see the open door of the bedroom right through the outline of the figure. Yet, the features and details of the human being were clearly visible.

Steed cried out in fear again because the transparent man was his father. The ghostly, otherworldly figure of Mr. Ryerson Gingert Steed stood in front of his son.

Steed could clearly see the facial features, the hair combed over to the side on top of the head; the wristwatch worn on the left wrist of the figure, the outline of shoes worn by the figure and the fact that the suit that the figure wore was the very suit that his son buried his father in. The handkerchief with his father's embroidered initials tucked into the suit jacket pocket was a sign. A distinct and telltale sign. Steed was there. At the funeral home, he selected the least expensive casket offered, because funerals were costly. He was there at the graveyard when they lowered the casket into the cold ground; he was there to sign the burial paperwork. Steed knew it all to be true.

Words emitted from the figure. The words came out of a mouth that actually moved in transparent edges, with just the slightest hints of the dying flames emitting from it.

"What verse comes next, Absalom?" The ghostly figure asked. Yes. It was indeed his father's voice.

At first, Steed could not find the strength to answer. His knees trembled in fear and his legs wobbled like bowling pins struck by a well-thrown ball. Then he slowly recovered as he convinced himself that this was all a dream. A nightmare. On the other hand, perhaps *he had* fallen ill. Yet, he was very frightened, as in a body trembling type of fright. Despite his fear, Steed still found the strength to dismiss what his eyes observed.

"You are not real. I can see right through you. This is just a dream or I am ill. Suffering from fever."

The outline of the figure instantly turned back into a burning flame and it burned with such an intensity that once more, Steed had to shield his eyes. To add to the horror, the figure screamed out in a blood-curdling scream that shook the dust and cobwebs out from the rafters of the home.

After screaming, the voice from the flame spoke again, "What is the next verse, my son? The verse!"

The voice echoed from out of the flames.

Again, Absalom Steed fell down upon his knees and lowered his head, and screamed out in fear and repentance, "I am sorry! So sorry, Father! To save us all from Satan's power! That is the next verse!"

The flame died away and the transparent outline of Ryerson Gingert Steed reappeared. This time, the manifestation had a much clearer outline of the facial features, while the rest of the body seemed to be spottier in details, with flames replacing the outlines of the figure. The figure of the elder Steed had human eyes that glared out at his son. The figure's eyes made Absalom Steed tremble even more while he deeply studied his father's eyes and he tried to comprehend what was actually happening here. These frightening eyes staring out at Absalom were the same shape as his own eyes and the same color. They were his father's eyes. No question. Absalom Steed knew his own father's eyes. He stared into them enough.

The figure spoke again, "Correct. You should heed the words, Absalom. Heed the warning of Satan's power. That is why I am here. That is why I arrived and you can see me. Arrived, today, on this blessed Christmas Day, even if I have been by your side, unseen and unheard most every day, most every hour, most every second of your life since I left this world."

The figure pointed to the radio. The radio stopped playing, and the song faded away slowly in volume until you could no longer hear it.

"You have been by my side, Father?"

"I have."

"Why couldn't I see you until now?"

"Because it was not allowed, and now, I appear before you in a form that you can see and with words that you can hear to give you a chance to escape what I could not escape."

Absalom felt a little more relaxed, as if he was having a conversation with his father. The reality of the recognition of his father's voice captured Absalom's mind. He stopped trembling so violently and stood up taller and a little steadier than he previously stood.

"Escape what?"

"My fate."

"Your fate? Father, why are you in immersed in flames? Are you banished to Hell?"

"No," the figure answered immediately, while its eyes rolled back in its ghostly head. The figure lifted its hands and cupped them to each side of the head, and the figure of Ryerson Gingert Steed shook its head violently back and forth. Before Absalom Steed could answer, the ghostly figure spoke in woeful cries of anguish. The words came out of its mouth in mournful cries that once more caused Absalom Steed to fall down on his knees and lower his head in trembles of fear.

"No! No! No! I am not in Hell. I was too evil, too sour, and too full of demented malice to be in Hell. I am in a much worse place. I would welcome Hell! I am in a place of torment and a place of observation of all the wretched aspects of this world, all the pain that I caused, all the suffering that I could have stopped. All the evil of the tapestry of deceit and ruthlessness that I alone wove!

I wander the world. I sit next to you, and watch and I have to exist in flames of heat, burning my senses in never ending pain and torment as I watch this world decay. I can never rest or escape the heat of the flames and the constant burn. I watch my own son, because of my teachings and evil lessons, weave his own tapestry of flames!"

Steed stood up again and his heart ached for his father's fate and at the meaning of his words.

"You taught me business, Father. Good business. You taught me what grandfather did wrong. You taught me how to change what he did wrong and you taught me to avenge what the doctors did to Mother. When they did not save her and stole her away from us." Steed held his hands out in front of his body in the figure's direction and with an open heart, Absalom Steed asked, "I do not understand. What did you do wrong?"

The figure of Ryerson Gingert Steed still held its hands on each side of its head and now gently shook its head back and forth while answering, "Everything. I did everything wrong. Your grandfather was such a good man. He warned me, and I foolishly did not heed his words. I dismissed my own father! I loved him so! I loved your mother so! I love you, my son! I turned dark and evil when your aunt and then mother left us and in a twisted response, I directed my anger and despair towards the world. My grave error was to use my great worldly wealth and power to destroy others. Innocent people suffered greatly because of my malice! I immersed our lives in business and in greed, and in cheating, and deceit, and undid all the good that my father did for this world. I punished the world because of my pain and I tarnished you, my son. Sent you to suffer the same fate as mine because your tapestry of evil and malice is a sturdy weave and woven with a powerful thread too."

Absalom Steed stood up rather shakily, and he stared at the figure of his father.

He recovered his thoughts and words from the ashes of his fear and said, "I love you too, dear Father! Dearly! You were and still are my life! Grandfather was right, and you were wrong? I need to ask, did my actions seal my ultimate fate already? Is there a chance for me to redeem my fate? Please tell me, dear Father. Why are you here? Why am I seeing you now and can interact with you, when previously, I could not?"

"There was an intervention of some sort. Of what I am not sure, but an intervention on your behalf and there is an allowance for me to be here, to warn you, to allow you to see me and be a witness to my terrible fate, to steer you so that you have a chance at escaping the power of Satan. Yes, your grandfather was right, and I was wrong. He was a great and powerful man. He loved Christmas so. You remember. Christmas celebrations here in this home were so joyful! So glorious! After today, you will remember so much more. My efforts at corruption buried the memories deep in your mind, but you remember. On this most holy of days, you will recall so much more. There is a chance for redemption, my son. A slim and faint chance. It is fleeting, but still valid. I am here because it is Christmas, my son. When you think that you have lost everything, Christmas, and the blessed Savior, arrives to save us all. That is the message! The purpose. The joy and the hope. Sadly, I chose to turn away from the message and my fate is what it is. Forever sealed to doom. You still have a chance! A chance at the joy and a chance to share the hope. I am so sorry for my actions and teachings. So, so sorry, my son. Please, heed the words and experiences to come, my son! I will capture some small solace at my being given a chance to save you from my horrible fate."

The figure waved frantically in the air with his hands in the direction of Absalom Steed, as if to emphasize the importance of his fading words.

"I must go now. Farewell, my beloved son! Farewell! Remember to heed. . ."

The voice slowly faded away as the figure dissolved into a flame. A small flame that burned slowly down until it faded into the darkness. Absalom Steed stood and watched as the flames burned down into a tiny ember and it disappeared before his eyes.

He rubbed at his eyes. Convinced that this was all a dream; in fact, a nightmare, he looked around into the now familiar darkness of the details of his bedroom and the cobwebs and dust and the foreboding, and then, in exhaustion, and with no thoughts of securing the door or the locks to his bedroom, Steed fell backwards into the bed, and quickly, Steed fell fast asleep.

Chapter Three
God Rest Ye Merry Gentlemen

ABSALOM WICKHAM STEED awoke to the blaring song on the radio. That same song. He opened his eyes wide and turned in anger to the radio, while muttering his now familiar label of, "Infernal Christmas. . .."

Yet, this time, unlike the others, he abruptly stopped short in his words. His eyes settled upon a person, or perhaps, a better and more accurate description was that it was not a person; it was a being of some sort standing next to his bed.

"God rest ye merry gentlemen, let nothing you dismay," slowly faded away.

Steed turned to watch the radio dial light fade away too. First, it glowed brightly and then it was dim, and then it faded away completely. It disappeared along with the melody and the music.

Steed turned his eyes and his attention to the being standing next to his bed. He was not afraid of, nor alarmed by, the being's presence. Perhaps, after the ghostly visit, or experience, or dream or whatever it actually was of the image of his father, he had grown used to strange apparitions, or perhaps, it was the appearance of the being that caused Steed no undue alarm.

In fact, the being invoked a welcoming presence. The being's resemblance was that of a man, an elderly man; it wore a long white robe with red lace trim along the hem, and along the cuffs, and the collar, and all the other edges of the robe. The face of the being was old, weathered, but kind. The being, had very bright and clear eyes and Steed could clearly see in the darkness of the bedroom that one eye was red, and one eye was green. It had a long white beard, and the being wore a red hat that seemed as if it was a wool hat made of the finest quality of wool that Steed had ever seen. The hat sat neatly upon the being's head, in a manner as if it was a teacup without a handle, turned upside down and placed upon its head. Above, the being's head hovered sprigs of bright green holly trimmed with bright red berries. The being was not tall, nor was the being short. It held its arms in front of its body and clasped its hands gently together as if it was preparing for prayer, while studying Absalom Steed carefully.

"Infernal Christmas, what, Mr. Steed? Did the visit of your father not teach you anything?" The being's voice asked in a melodious voice that seemed as if it floated upon the bars of a Christmas melody. The voice was extremely comforting and soothing. Absalom Steed sat up in his bed, pulled the bedcovers up around him and studied the being standing in front of him.

After clearing his throat, Steed answered the question rather hesitantly at first, and then he gathered some confidence, "I am not sure what is happening. I am not sure if I am dreaming or if I am ill and feverish or just in a daze. Furthermore, just in case this is not a dream, or a fever or a daze, I rather not say anything further within the perception of a negative context about Christmas because I am afraid that you might hold it against me in your purpose. I see that you have some strong affiliation with the holiday. At least, if the holly and the berries, and the attire and your overall appearance are an accurate sign thereof. Not to mention the unique Christmas-like colors of your eyes. Am I correct in my assumption?"

"You are," the being answered and added, "I assure you that I will hold nothing against you. My visit only means you a fleeting chance at redemption, and I know all about you, Mr. Steed. I too, as your father has been, have been at your side for a very long time. We have been together every Christmas Day since you were born. Therefore, that makes this Christmas Day the forty-first celebration that we have shared together. However, I must admit that the last twenty-two years of our celebrations have not been very joyous. You have chosen to ignore me, yet, when we were young together, we celebrated rather gleefully."

"Gleefully? Celebrations? I have never seen you or met you before this night or day or dream, or whatever it is."

"Yes, I understand that you perceive what is happening right now as blurred and tainted. That is because of the hardening of your heart is to the extent that makes it virtually impenetrable, Mr. Steed. I just said that we have been together every Christmas Day since you were born. Since I was born too. We stood side-by-side every Christmas Day."

Steed tossed his bedcovers aside and stood up next to his bed.

"Okay, well, that may or may not be comforting. Do you have a name, a title, or a purpose? I feel as if this is a familiar story of sorts. I am part of that same old story, too. You know, the three spirits, the mean, old miser, and such."

"Ha! You might be! An excellent reference, Mr. Steed. Yet, if we compare you to Mr. Dickens's fictional character, you are much worse. Much, much worse. Unfortunately, for this world, you are real and fortunately, for this world, Scrooge was not. This weary world could not tolerate two of you!"

Steed noticed that an aura of bright red, green, and blue lights, or rather, it was more of a hue, now appeared around the being as the being spoke to Mr. Steed. The aura burned brighter, and it seemed to ebb and flow with the emotions and the impact of the words of the being.

Gracefully, the being glided to the side of the bed, very close to Mr. Steed while continuing to explain, "Except that today, on this blessed Christmas Day, there are no other ghosts, or visits, or spirits. Only me."

Steed's pointy ears twitched a little as he waved toward the being and asked, "And you are?"

"For simplicity's sake, let us just call me the Spirit of Christmas."

Absalom Steed quickly reverted to his business executive ways in his reply, "Okay, you are a manager of all of the spirit of Christmas? That seems as if it is a monumental task. I hope that whoever, or whatever, pays you very well for your efforts. After all, Christmas has now become quite the commercial mess. The sales, the waste, the money, the. . .."

Steed stopped short in his words when he saw the Spirit of Christmas shaking his head back and forth, and then he pointed at Absalom Steed and spoke, "No. Did you not learn anything from the lament of your father? This world is not about money, wealth, and putting a price tag on everything and everyone. No, I only am concerned with your Christmas, and your redemption, Mr. Steed."

"Are you an angel or something similar, Spirit of Christmas?"

"Oh no, no, no. I could never reach that status. I am what I say that I am. The Spirit of Christmas. That works out best for both of us."

Steed waved his hands toward the Spirit and rudely dismissed his presence. His meanness would not leave just because of a few simple visions and visits from beings of other worlds!

"Well, that is very cheery. Good luck to you. I must request that you leave now from this dream. I rather just go back to bed and rise early. I have important numbers to study all day tomorrow."

The aura grew brighter and brighter and the Spirit of Christmas smiled widely, took a few steps, and then walked next to where Steed stood and sat down in the air on an invisible support, crossed his legs and spoke, "Numbers, always numbers, Mr. Steed. Why do you think this is a dream? Are you sure of it?"

"Of course, it is a dream. I do not partake of wine or whiskey or beer because they are very costly and frivolous. I am not feverish, so the only conclusion that I can draw is that this is merely a dream. My father's appearance was a nightmare, and this part is now the happy part of the dream. All of these spurious thoughts and emotions and visions brought on by that silly, feeble-minded manager of mine, Mr. Wesley Shook, and his allowance of that blasted radio, and stealing of my gifts, and endless babble of infernal Christmas drivel. In fact, your very title, I picked up in my sub-conscious from Shook's stupid radio program. The Spirit of Christmas. Ha! Yes! That is the only explanation."

The aura dimmed a little, and the spirit continued to sit in the air while speaking, "My goodness. We are back to the infernal Christmas talk. You certainly are something else, Mr. Steed. Blaming poor Wesley Shook for invoking emotions." The Spirit of Christmas pointed to the radio on the table and added, "Not to mention that you took another man's property for your own! That radio is invaluable. As it has so aptly demonstrated."

Steed whirled around to look at the radio and then to the Spirit.

His ears twitched and his beady eyes narrowed as he replied, "It is rightfully mine! It is contraband rightfully seized and confiscated on my private property! Not allowed in my factory! That soft-shoe, cupcake, Shook allowed it. They broke the rules. Not Absalom Steed!"

"Ha! Contraband! It is a radio, not contraband. Rules, Mr. Steed? Your rules? Isn't it always about your endless rules, Mr. Steed? Okay, I can see that we need to show you visions. Many visions to penetrate the hardness of your heart and mind. It is time to go now. Grab your winter robe there—off the bedpost because you might catch a chill. This weary world does not need you any colder than you already are."

The Spirit of Christmas stood up and he floated a little in the air and the aura grew bright and powerful and the colors captivated, Mr. Steed. Steed found himself lost in the vision and magic of the colors.

"Go? Go to where?" Absalom Steed asked as he donned his winter robe.

"To see what we will see. To find the joy and hope and peace of Christmas that you once knew and loved, that we shared together and you somehow lost. To recover your soul, Mr. Steed."

The words of the Spirit of Christmas negated Steed's formerly impenetrable defenses. He nodded at the words, while still studying the beauty of the aura.

"Come along now. Let us visit your Christmas, Mr. Steed. We only have limited time. Take my hand. We have many miles and adventures to cover, not to mention a fleeting chance at redemption to capture."

Steed reached out and touched the hand of the Spirit of Christmas, and in a blink of an eye, Steed found himself spinning uncontrollably in the air. Around and around, he went while he firmly held onto the hand of the Spirit of Christmas. Then, with a thud and a slight bounce, they landed upright on their feet.

Absalom Steed realized that he closed his eyes at some point during their journey and he was loudly screaming. When he opened his eyes, he was standing next to the Spirit of Christmas in the grand entrance foyer of his home.

Only it was not as it was now. Gone were the dust and the dullness and the darkness.

The interior of the home was warm and cozy and brightly illuminated with candles, and with Christmas lights, and the magnificent glass crystal chandeliers glowed in brilliance. Everywhere you looked were Christmas and holiday decorations. There were glorious sprigs of holly adorned with plump red berries, and freshly cut and formed evergreen wreaths that smelled better than warm peanut butter hung on the doors and on the walls. Mistletoe balls and decorations with golden bells in their centers waited for lucky lovers and hung from the doorways and in strategic locations on lower parts of the ceilings. Finely woven throw rugs woven into magnificent patterns and intricate details by the finest artisans and imported from Nottingham, England, were underfoot in the foyer. Seasonally decorated tables stood around the perimeter of the room. Some tables contained liquor bottles, wine, champagne, and beer. Standing at attention on the table were assortments of fine glassware ready to serve the drinks and refreshments. Other tables mounded with pastries, cookies, slices of the finest cuts of various types of meats and there were slices of cheeses and hors d'oeuvres and starter foods of all types imaginable. And the centerpiece of it all was a magnificent Christmas tree set at the base of the stunning and elegant center staircase leading to the upper reaches of the mansion. The tree was fresh cut and even amid the supernatural vision; its aroma was glorious and tickled Steed's senses. The tree towered at least ten or more feet above the floor. Glass and wooden Christmas ornaments of every kind, color, shape, and size adorned the tree and what seemed as if it were hundreds, maybe even a thousand glowing red, green, and blue bulbs perched on strings of Christmas lights glowed from the branches. A garland that seemed made of pieces of gold spiraled down the tree from top to bottom, each twist and turn carefully placed so it was magnificent in its presentation and perfectly symmetrical in its journey. On the tippy-top of the tree stood a silver and gold, illuminated star that when Absalom Steed looked upon it, its brilliance seemed to borrow deep into his eyes and the image remained there even when he blinked. Underneath the tree chugged an O gauge electric train, rolling merrily and mightily around the perimeter of the base of the tree, making its way through a small replica of a Christmas village. A village filled with miniature houses, a church, miniature village people, and a downtown area.

The entire scene was breathtaking, and Absalom Steed did not mince words. His eyes were wide and open and he looked up at the scene and the tree and took in every detail. Steed's pointy ears twitched in excitement, yet he still resisted a smile.

"Why, it is my home, our home, the Steed mansion at Christmastime. On Christmas Eve! Yes! I remember this! I do! I do! Christmas was so glorious! Every Christmas Eve, my grandfather hosted a magnificent Christmas party here at the Steed mansion. My grandfather, he so loved Christmas, and he spared no expense to make it a magnificent time! Look at that tree! Look at all of the food and drink and the wreaths and the holly filled with those glorious red berries. All real too! No artificial decorations for Mr. Gerald Lambert Steed and the Steed family! You can smell their glorious evergreen aromas! No, no, no! Only the finest and the best! Look upon it all, Spirit of Christmas!"

The Spirit of Christmas turned and watched Absalom Steed, and the Spirit smiled at his reaction.

The Spirit's melodious voice filled the room, "I see it and recall it, too. Remember, I was here, too. And so were your family and you. Yes, he spared no expense, Mr. Steed. A lesson that you seemed to forget. Apparently, your grandfather did not hide away pocket change and extra dollars in hidden wall safes. Money means very little when compared to happiness, love, joy, and memories, Mr. Steed. The gold seems like sand when we compare it to this!"

The Spirit waved his arms in the air in a graceful sweeping motion and the scene came alive even more, because now, in a blink of an eye, the scene filled with people! The aura of Christmas colors glowed brighter than ever before above the Spirit's head, but now, when Steed gazed upon it, his beady eyes did not shut, they opened wider than ever and he did not have to shield his eyes from the brilliance of the colors as he previously did. It was as if Steed's eyes slowly absorbed the colors.

When Absalom Steed looked away from the aura of colors and turned his gaze upon the scene, he smiled widely. His face almost cracked from the force of it. Steed finally smiled, and that had not occurred in many, many years. He broke his vow of never smiling again and he seemed thrilled to do so!

"Why, it is my grandfather! There he is. And my father and my dear, dear, mother. My mother! Look how handsome the men are, Spirit! Look how beautiful my dear mother is! Look! They are all alive. However, how is this so, Spirit of Christmas? How is this so?"

The Spirit looked at Steed and his smile was wide and powerful, too.

As his melodious voice explained, "Our loved ones never die, Mr. Steed. These are your memories and they are always in your mind. You just hid them away to hide your pain. You tucked them under the cover of layers upon layers of anger and meanness and bitterness. However, they are always there. We are just visiting them because of my arrival today. The Spirit of Christmas. When you allow me in your life and in your heart, you can always access their love."

Steed nodded at the explanation and he continued to point out the people in the scene, and his exuberance grew and grew.

Mr. Gerald Lambert Steed was, indeed, a very handsome man. He was tall and his shoulders were wide and his waist was narrow. He had round eyes that glowed in a clear blue that, while he stood next to his magnificent Christmas tree, reflected the many colors of the decorations in those same eyes. He had a well-trimmed, neat beard and perfectly groomed salt and pepper hair that very much resembled his grandson's present hair color. In fact, as Absalom Steed stood smiling at the scene, it seemed as if the two men's features began to show a unique resemblance. Absalom's features grew less pointy, his ears did not twitch, his eyes grew rounder and wider and his smile actually made his face blush and he was not as pale.

Gerald Steed wore a fine brown tweed suit, custom tailored to fit his lean and powerful body, and he wore a matching vest with a collared shirt and a silky necktie. On his feet, he wore highly polished brown shoes. You could see the reflections of the Christmas tree lights in the polish of the shoes. Nothing was out of place on the man. Nothing at all.

Ryerson Gingert Steed stood next to his father and, he too, was very handsome and proud. The resemblance was keen and profound, yet there were differences between the father and his son. Ryerson's eyes were a dark brown. He was just a little shorter than his father was and his dark brown hair was thick and combed over to the side in delicate waves. He was clean-shaven and his face was a little longer than his father's face was, but just as handsome. Ryerson also wore a perfectly tailored suit; a brown suit that was one solid brown color throughout, even on the lapels, and he wore a silky necktie made of the finest materials.

Then, there standing next to Ryerson Steed was Absalom's mother! Oh, what a beautiful woman she was!

Emily Belle Steed was stunning. Her presence and elegance and beauty lit up an entire room on its own. There was no need for any further illumination when Mrs. Steed was present. Her hair was a striking strawberry red, and it tumbled down her back and over her shoulders in graceful, curly waves. She was captivating and statuesque, and while she wore a conservative red dress, the dress still displayed her glorious figure. Around her neck, she wore a string of white pearls that matched white pearl earrings. Her perfect facial features and a million-dollar smile helped to turn everyone's heads in the room as the crowd gathered around the Christmas tree in the foyer and watched as Mrs.

Steed stood proudly next to her husband while they locked their arms together in unity. They made a striking couple.

"Look, Spirit! Please look at the dignities gathered here," Absalom Steed pointed out as his eyes scanned the scene in front of them, "these are all very important persons in Paterson and in New Jersey. Bankers, doctors, lawyers, business owners, look, there is the Mayor of Paterson and his wife, and there, is the Bishop of the Newark Diocese, and the Bishop of Paterson and even Rabbi Goldberg from the temple over on the east side." Steed turned and nodded at the Spirit and added with enthusiasm to his observations, "This is not even a holiday that the rabbi observes! My grandfather commanded such a presence! He was very important, you know."

"He was, and in fact, still is, Mr. Steed. I hope you realize his impact on your life, and many other lives. My broadcasts of Christmas are of joy, love, and hope to reach out to all persons, who care to listen, Mr. Steed. The actual meaning of Christmas is love. It knows no boundaries of religion, or of prejudice, because love penetrates everything."

Steed carefully studied the Spirit through his ever-widening eyes, and he nodded in acknowledgment of the words.

Servers dressed in black formal attire milled about, serving food and drinks, and taking orders for the same.

And in the adjoining room, a string quartet provided musical entertainment. The lovely notes of Christmas music floated through the mansion. Suddenly, dashing in through one of the side-doorways, a lovely woman, red-faced and beaming she was, with her auburn hair flowing behind her and a mile-wide smile on her face, made a bounding entrance into the room.

"I am here! I am here! So sorry, dear Father. I was tuning my violin and playing a bit. Preparing to play for everyone!" The woman buried deeply into the chest and outstretched arms of Mr. Gerald Steed, who hugged her tightly and warmly and laughed at her apologies and bursting onto the scene.

"No, sorry, ever! My dear daughter, always rushing around and bringing joy to everywhere she is!"

"Why it is Auntie Marilynn!" Absalom Steed excitedly announced while remaining slightly flabbergasted and overwhelmed at the unfolding scene. Yet, Absalom Steed remained clearly enthralled at the replaying of the memories, and the visions, and the rebirth of his loved ones. Steed stood and pointed out the persons in front of them to the Spirit of Christmas.

Marilynn Dorothy Steed resembled the rest of the family in facial features and in style and grace, yet she was not tall and lean like her brother and her father were. Instead, she was shorter, a little rounder, and her face was full and her complexion danced with a splattering of fascinating freckles. She was quite the beauty.

"She could have been a concert violinist, playing within great and prestigious circles in the musical world, Spirit. She was so talented. She could have been. Instead, she gave up a chance at musical greatness to work in social causes. In Catholic and ecumenical charities in the heart of the inner city here in Paterson. She helped many poor families through troublesome times. Auntie Marilynn was so kind and gentle. I loved her dearly. She taught me to play the violin. She was patient and loving with me."

"The violin, Mr. Steed. Very interesting. Such a gentle instrument for such an imposing and harsh man to play. You were quite the player too."

"I was. Yes, indeed, I was."

"Do you still play?"

"No. I never played again after Auntie Marilynn died. I could not even ever look upon the instrument. It was too painful. She left us all too soon. As did so many of my loved ones. Gone too soon," Steed said.

The Spirit observed how he clenched his hands into fists and bit his teeth together so hard that his temples pounded.

"Yes, I agree, Mr. Steed. She was quite the kind soul and contributed much good will and joy to this weary world. Rest assured that her place in Heaven is glorious. She died before any marriage. Correct?"

"Yes, she had many suitors. One young man won her heart. He worked at the lace factory. Auntie Marilynn knew no social or other boundaries. He was one of the best machine operators. A lead man on the floor. Very skilled. Martin Shaw was his name. They became engaged shortly before she fell ill. It was a very difficult time for him and for all of us. Her death was a shock and a great loss to this world and to my family and to Mr. Shaw. He was an outstanding man. I remember him well."

The aura grew dimmer above the head of the Spirit as he rubbed his long beard.

The Spirit stared in at Steed and said, "Shaw, huh? Is that not the same family that your present operator, one of your best employees, a certain Mr. Jonathan Shaw, is a descendant of? Is that not Mr. Shaw's radio on your end table in your bedroom?"

Steed unclenched his fists and lowered his head as shame and guilt built within his soul. Recognition of your own poor behavior is never easy, and for Steed, it was like cracking solid concrete with a fork.

"It is Martin's grandson. He too, is very talented."

Satisfied with Steed's reaction, the Spirit continued to quiz Steed in an effort to open his beady eyes a little wider and smooth the edges of his pointedness.

"Auntie Marilynn resembles your grandmother? No?"

"She did, she did. I only have very faint memories of my grandmother. She too, gone too soon."

"Kidney disease. Was it not, Mr. Steed?"

"It was, yes. It is an awful disease. Back in that day and time, doctors just began with examining the potential for kidney transplants. I doubt that they could even find a suitable donor for a kidney because we have very rare blood types in our bloodline. I could have been a match. Perhaps. Who knows? I would have given Auntie Marilynn both of my kidneys if I could have because I loved her so much. However, I was too young, and the technology did not exist back then for such operations. It is a curse to the Steed family. A curse. Took them all. Ironically and horribly, it took my own dear mother, too. A transplant is not always a cure, Spirit. The disease is very powerful."

The Spirit spotted just a rim of tears in the eyes of Steed and forced his recognition thereof by pointing at the tears and saying, "I see the manifestation of your grief and I truly sympathize. Did your family not use their wealth to fight back at the disease? To make a difference?"

"They did and the disease won and we lost."

"Kidney disease won, huh? Just as Mrs. Worrall is suffering through right now? Oh well, what part of all of that is your problem, Mr. Steed?" The Spirit tossed Steed's own words and his meanness and malice right back at him now; and the impact of his harshness and the realization of the depth of his malice forced Steed to display his emotions even more. The tears rimmed his beady eyes a little more, finally forcing Steed to reach up with his fingers and wipe at them.

"I see your methods now, Spirit. You are using my own words now to force trapped tears to surface and to inflict self-examination, Spirit. My own words."

"Your words, Mr. Steed. Not mine. Your words are a power that you yield, a way to injure and demean and control. As you seek redemption, then, in the future, choose your words and actions carefully. Mr. Steed, take a lesson from your grandfather and look again at his actions and listen to his words!"

They turned back to the scene unfolding before them and the aura returned to its brilliance as the colors danced and bounced above, in, and around, the Spirit of Christmas.

"Where is our Absalom?" Gerald Steed asked his daughter.

"Oh, he was with me, we were playing a bit," Marilynn Steed explained, and then she turned and called out to the other room, "Abbie! Abbie! Come in now. Your grandfather is going to speak!"

A tall, lean young man, a pre-teen, rushed into the foyer, full of energy and life. He shouted while he dashed, and the crowd of on-lookers laughed and cheered at his excitement.

"I am coming! I am here, Auntie Marilynn, Father, Mother, Grandfather! I am here!"

The Spirit of Christmas playfully elbowed Absalom Steed in his side while teasing him about his nickname.

"Abbie? My goodness, you were her little favorite."

Absalom smiled again and once more, some tears rimmed his eyes as he watched the shadows and visions of him in his youth rush to join his family. Young Absalom's hair was thick and longish, and he wore a suit and a necktie too. His shoes made a clickity-clack noise as he hustled across the floors to make his way to the foyer. In many ways, he was a youthful version of his father and grandfather, but in some of his facial features, you could see a strong resemblance to his mother. Young Absalom rushed to his father's side. He squeezed between his parents, folded his hands in front of his body and smiled widely at his favorable position.

Absalom viewed the scene with raw emotions.

"Yes, I loved her so. She loved me, too. Yes, Auntie Marilynn, always called me Abbie. My dear mother would too, occasionally, use that nickname to address me." And, his voice lowered and choked a little before the words arrived, "One other person called me Abbie too. I loved them all dearly. I had a wonderful life as a youngster. Much love afforded to me. Look, there, Spirit. I am quite handsome too and such a head of hair that I had! Tall for my age. I recall all of this quite well now. It is coming back to me vividly. I am around eleven or twelve years of age here. It is Christmas of nineteen-forty-five. Right after the war ended. Grandfather is to make an important announcement now."

Absalom turned and faced the Spirit, and now he focused intently upon the moment, as if they were viewing a television program.

Steed put his finger to his mouth and whispered, "Please. Let us be quiet now and listen."

The Spirit of Christmas nodded and smiled at Steed's instructions and reaction. The colors of the aura surrounding the Spirit glowed brightly and steadily as Mr. Gerald Lambert Steed cleared his throat and waved his arms in the air.

His voice was powerful and confident, and a quiet hush settled in over the attendees as they directed their attention to Mr. Steed. Even the servers stood and listened as he addressed the gathering.

"Good evening. Hello. Honored guests, my friends, and my family, thank you for attending our annual Christmas gathering. It is truly my honor to have you here in our home as we celebrate the joy of Christmas and the end of the horrors of war. While it was an awful and tumultuous time for our country and our allies, we celebrate our victory of the free world, and all of us, at Steed Lace, are proud of our role in that victory. Partnering with our friends and counterparts in England, Scotland, Ireland, and Wales, we produced lace and garments for the war effort. Contributing boot laces, and parachute parts and uniforms, jackets, and gloves for our troops and to be a part of a team that defeated evil and hatred in our world!"

All the attendees clapped and cheered and celebrated the words of Mr. Steed.

With gestures of gratitude, Mr. Steed acknowledged the applause and when the crowd quieted, Mr. Steed continued, "We were fortunate to have a solid workforce in place during the war and our employees who served, all returned home safely to us and for that we thank God with praise and gratitude."

There was more applause and Absalom Steed looked on while remaining smiling and captivated by the words and power of his grandfather.

"Now, as we move forward, and rebuild our lives, our country, and the world, I am proud to announce a new initiative. The Steed Foundation. It will be a not-for-profit entity, organized, and led by my daughter, Marilynn Dorothy Steed and assisted by her brother, my son, Ryerson Gingert Steed. The Steed Foundation will assist those in need in our great city and throughout New Jersey and beyond, through job retraining for returning veterans, job corps, assisting the poor and destitute in our communities in finding affordable health care, assisting in medical needs during catastrophic illness and other charity functions. And our first project will be the construction of new wings inside of our downtown hospitals. New wings, with the best medical equipment, the best nurses, and doctors. All dedicated to fighting kidney disease and other horrible disorders and diseases and providing the best state-of-the-art medical care for kidney disease patients and support for the families. We will name these wings in memorial for my wife, the late Mrs. Cora Wickham Steed, who lost her brave battle to that same wretched disease five years ago. Initially, I will fund the construction projects with my own money and I know everyone in this generous community will join in, as together we work as a team to make our city and all the persons here, healthier, and more prosperous and to improve the quality of lives for everyone! God bless America and merry Christmas to all!"

The crowd of party gatherers erupted in wild applause and in a joyous celebration. They shared a champagne toast and when the clergymen in attendance extended some blessings, it was the rabbi who blessed the host of the party. Rabbi Goldberg moved to the front of the crowd and held his arms out to join in unison as he blessed the efforts, the life, and the visions of Mr. Gerald Lambert Steed.

After the toast and blessings, Mr. Gerald Steed thanked everyone again and continued to speak, "Please let the celebration continue. I invite you to enjoy the food and the drink and enjoy a special treat in the library as Marilynn shares her special musical talents and she plays beautiful Christmas music on her violin. . .."

During the replaying of the entire scene of his past, Mr. Absalom Steed remained mesmerized and as the crowd moved off to listen to the performance and Steed and the Spirit followed, the gentle notes of the music sounded as if they floated from Heaven afar.

"Infernal Christmas music," the Spirit whispered to Absalom, who hung his head in shame at the pain in his words and the lack of honor on his aunt's joy of music and his own joy, too.

"The Steed Foundation," the Spirit of Christmas reminded Absalom, "created as a vision by your grandfather. A great man, a great visionary and human being and a good and worthy organization, which saved and provided for many needy people, yet your father dismantled it all."

"He had his reasons, Spirit. Good reasons," Absalom defended his father's actions.

The Spirit did not comment on the response, but instead, he waved his arms in the air and spoke in his usual melodious voice, "Come, Mr. Steed. Look upon this scene no longer. We have another vision to see, another Christmas to revisit, and more lessons to learn! Hold my hand tightly!"

Steed reached out and touched the hand of the Spirit of Christmas, and in a blink of an eye, Steed once again found himself spinning uncontrollably in the air. Around and around, he went while he clung to the hand of the Spirit of Christmas. Then, with a thud and a slight bounce, they landed again, upright on their feet.

When Absalom Steed opened his eyes, he found that they stood off to the side of the large production area of the Steed Lace Factory. A production area that, mostly, looked similar to how it was now in the present day, with a few exceptions. A brightly illuminated Christmas tree sat on the production floor, some Christmas wreaths and other decorations adorned the walls and other locations throughout the production floor, and the machines were all shutdown, oiled by the maintenance mechanics and covered with cloths. Presently, there was no production occurring. To top the scene off with some Christmas magic, a radio played some soft "infernal Christmas music" as it happily sat on a table in the far corner of the production floor. The team of production workers all gathered around in the front of the production floor underneath the management offices and the viewing windows; the very same windows that Mr. Absalom Steed stared out of just a few scant hours earlier. His grandfather, dressed and looking immaculate, albeit a little older and thinner than in the previous vision, stood at the front of the team and an older Absalom Steed stood nearby next to his father. Ryerson Steed did not look happy. In fact, he folded his arms across his chest in a display of some defiance and dismay as to what he was witnessing.

Mr. Gerald Steed spoke, and out of respect for the speech, a worker ran and turned down the music on the radio.

"Hello and merry Christmas Eve! On this most joyous day, we want to thank you for another banner year! Thank you for all your hard work and efforts in contributing to our mutual success! In gratitude of your efforts we have free turkeys and hams to give to each of you for enjoyment this holiday season, as well as fifty-dollar United States Savings Bonds for each worker, and," the workers began to cheer and applaud and Mr. Steed smiled and waved his hands in the air for them to stop and listen, "and, and, thank you, and since we are ahead on our production and shipping in advance, we will shut down the shop and factory production from now until after New Year's Day with full pay for all shifts!"

The aura of colors burned brightly over the head and all around the Spirit of Christmas as the Spirit, too, applauded and cheered the vision. Steed stood and watched, but his reaction was far less excited.

"You do not look so happy, then and now, Mr. Steed. Neither did your father. Why so? The generosity of your grandfather and his Christmas spirit overflows."

"It does, it does. No question that he was a kind, wonderful, and generous man. Perhaps, too much so. I do not know." Steed said while he pointed at his younger self in the vision. "I recall this Christmas Eve very vividly. I am just seventeen or eighteen here. Just learning the business and my father felt that my grandfather was running the business astray. The paid time off, the free turkeys and hams, the savings bonds, and I will tell you a secret, kind Spirit, we actually lost money that year for the first time in forever. My grandfather spent more and more time at the foundation work and less at the factory and loaned the foundation a great deal of cash to sustain the projects when some donors dried up. It was a difficult time. To top it all off, my grandfather, my aunt, and my mother's health declined after that Christmas and everything changed. It seemed as if the end of the prosperous and joyous era for the Steed family began after that Christmas. My father grew bitter towards my grandfather and they slowly grew apart and sadly became . . . estranged. It was . . . terrible. They were so close at one time. I think it contributed to my grandfather's heart issues and his untimely death. His heart broke at the situation and the changes in my father." Steed's voice crackled as he spoke with the emotion, he then stopped speaking and narrowed his eyes on the scene and the vision before them.

A worker ran over and turned the radio up, and the Christmas music floated loudly through the factory. Smartly dressed servers passed food, beer, and wine around and a rollicking Christmas Eve party was now underway. In the vision, Ryerson Steed beckoned to his son and the two of them retreated to the office to pour over the numbers and the books, whereas Steed's grandfather joined in the celebration.

"I know all these men. All these workers, Spirit of Christmas. They were all exceptional workers that produced the finest quality products and took pride in doing so. Loyal men. Proud and dedicated. They are all gone now. I think. I imagine that they are all dead and gone by now. I don't exactly know. I do recall all their names."

Absalom Steed pointed and called the names of the workers out as he identified them by his memories, "There is Martin Shaw, and Billy O'Leary and James Smith. Quinton Taylor and Wallace Hannah, Timothy Whitehouse, Casey Davis," and on and on, Mr. Absalom Steed went until he identified each and every worker.

When Steed finished, the Spirit watched as Absalom Steed took a deep breath and his eyes, which had been less beady and were rounder during the previous vision, narrowed once more. The Spirit made careful note of his behavior.

Finally, the Spirit asked, "What are you thinking, Mr. Steed?"

"I am thinking that I wish I had handled the radio and the gifts incident today a little better than I did, Spirit. That I wish . . . to speak to Mr. Wesley Shook a little too. Explain some things."

The Spirit reached out his hand and said, "I understand, Mr. Steed. Focus not upon your regrets, Mr. Steed. Instead, focus upon your redemption. Come along. There are many more miles to travel and our time is growing shorter and shorter."

Steed nodded and clasped hands with the Spirit of Christmas and once more, they spun off together to the next adventure.

ABSALOM WICKHAM STEED opened his eyes when he felt his feet touch the ground, or the floor, or the Earth. Wherever it was now that the Spirit had led them to.

Upon scanning his surroundings, he immediately knew where he was. It looked the same, and the pain he felt then was the same pain that he felt now. He cupped his hands to his face and shook his head.

He looked over at his companion and guide and said in a low voice that carried an air of intense sadness to it, "Oh please, Spirit. Not here. Why here? Anywhere but here. Can we just skip this over?"

"No, Mr. Steed. I am sorry, but with the joy of every life, there comes considerable pain, too. To work towards your redemption, you need to understand what caused your waywardness to begin with. Look here. See where you are and what was then."

In an effort to comfort Absalom Steed, the Spirit of Christmas gently touched the shoulder of Steed and rested his hand firmly upon it.

The aura grew very dim above the head of the Spirit and it seemed as if sadness crept into the Spirit's demeanor, too. The scene slowly unfolded before them as they watched. A scene at the downtown hospital, in a private room, in the wing named for Absalom's grandmother, and the younger Absalom stood next to the hospital bed while in the hallway outside, his father's voice raged in anger laced with grief. A beautiful young woman sat on a chair next to the bed, tears streaming down her cheeks. A body was still in the bed. The body was underneath covers pulled up over the entire body, even covering the head of the body lying there in front of Absalom and the young woman. No medical equipment monitors beeped or lights flashed on the hospital equipment. All the power to the equipment was now off. Ominously silent.

"That's it! It is over, Doctor Lawton! Over! I want my mother's name removed from this wing by the end of this day. The Steed Foundation is not funding anything here as far as research goes, and in fact . . . I will resolve to dissolve the Steed Foundation as soon as I can."

Ryerson Steed's voice raged throughout the hospital.

"Please, Mr. Steed, I know your grief is powerful, and you are understandably very upset, but there are many patients resting here, and please, you need to calm down. Perhaps, we can go to my office and discuss this in private."

"Private! Ha! Resting. Yes, my wife is resting now too, you idiot! No, I want the entire hospital to know of your incompetence. First, my sister died under your care, now my wife, and you allowed them both to die! All the money, all the begging and the same results."

The voice of Ryerson Steed was loud and unruly and raging.

"Please, Mr. Steed, in my defense, it was an aggressive form of the disease and the transplant rejected so soon, too. Too soon for her body to recover. Her blood type, just as your sister's blood type was, made it a difficult transplant situation. Transplants are not cures, Mr. Steed. We have so much more research to do to understand this disease. We tried everything. I assure you. Mrs. Steed asked us to stop the treatments. I begged her to continue with the treatments, but she wished to stop."

"Done! Conversation over. The gravy train ends here, doctor. You stole your last penny from the Steed Foundation and from my family and from me!"

Inside the private room, the beautiful young woman dabbed at her tears with a tissue. She stood up, and she walked over to the younger version of Absalom Steed and gently touched him on his right shoulder.

She spoke in a sweet, low voice laced with the residues of her sobs, "Come now, Abbie. Please, let's go and see your father and comfort him. He is so upset. Do you hear his cries of pain and of grief? His voice is so loud, and he is angry with my father." The younger version of Absalom Steed's face grew angry, and his round eyes narrowed with pain and fierceness. He spun around and angrily tore her hand from his shoulder.

His words came out with harshness and bitterness, "Do I hear his cries of pain and grief? Of course, I do. This is his wife and my dear mother's cold, lifeless body underneath these covers, lying here dead. Do you take me for a fool?"

"Abbie, no, of course not. Please. I love you dearly. With all of my heart and my soul. . .."

Surprised at his anger, the young woman took a few steps back and then she went to reach out her arms to embrace Absalom Steed, but the young man in the vision blocked her embrace and tossed her arms aside while speaking once more, "No! I don't want your sympathy. I don't want you or anything to do with you or your father, or this place or your family. Most of all, I do not want you and your supposed love."

While watching the scene unfold of his past, and obviously knowing what occurs next in the vision in front of them, the present version of Absalom Steed, put his hands over his face and pleaded with the Spirit of Christmas, "Please, kind Spirit. Please let us go. I cannot bear to watch this any longer. Please have some pity and mercy on me and take me away from this wretched place."

"Life is full of joy and some sorrow, too. Watch this, Absalom. Watch and recall the source of your bitterness. Betty Anne Lawton loved you so. She was, and in fact, still is, sincere beyond words with her proclamation of love. Her heart was yours. Out of grief, bitterness, and mourning, you turned her away. Your father and you unfairly blamed her father for your mother's death and the death of Auntie Marilynn, too. Marilynn inherited the same disease from your grandmother. Your dear mother's illness was a horrible twist of fate. Part of a journey, I am afraid. Doctor Lawson was a great doctor and he saved many lives with his outstanding dedication to his work. He was not incorrect in his treatments, and he really did his best. You unfairly blamed poor Betty Anne, and she was guilty of only one thing, and that was of falling in love with you! No, we will not leave, because it is out of love that I appeared to you this Christmas, while in other past Christmases, I stood by your side, invisible and silent, yet still on a mission of love. God stands by your side, stands by us all, Mr. Steed. Yet, often God is silent in words but powerful in actions, but God's love is all around you. You just need to place aside your bitterness and open your heart to accept it. Uncover your eyes and watch."

The Spirit of Christmas waved his arms in the air. Absalom Steed's hands fell away from his face and the cover of his eyes, and he was powerless either to move his arms, or his hands, or to shut his eyes. Steed's younger self raged at the sobbing Betty Anne Lawton as her tears fell like rain.

The vision of the young Absalom Steed loudly proclaimed the end of their relationship, "Consider our engagement broken! Ended! Over! I would not be able to be with you or even look at you again, or your father, or your mother, or your family! Your father's empty promises. His wishful thinking, his meaningless words. He told us there was a chance to beat the disease with a transplant and treatments, and yet, my mother died!"

"He did all that he could, Absalom. Your mother wished for the treatments to end. Her body grew too weak to continue and the treatments and her condition ravaged her quality of life. My father is not God. You are not thinking clearly. Your grief is profound."

Young Absalom Steed shook his head violently and shouted, "Oh, no. I am thinking very clearly. I see what you are and what your father is. Takers. Our money is your goal. Build more hospital wings, buy more and more useless equipment, and obtain more prestige for your family at the expense of mine. My father is correct. This is to end. No, I was not thinking clearly, when I asked you to be my wife. There is no love here. I don't love you. Give me the ring back. Give. Me. The. Ring. Now."

His fists curled in rage as Betty Anne tugged at the diamond engagement ring on her finger and pulled it off and between sobs, said, "As you wish. Here."

The present-day Absalom yelled at his former self, "You fool! Give the ring back to her. Stop! Tell her how much you love her! See your errors. Don't listen to your father's grief! She was glorious. The best thing that you ever had! Fool! Fool!"

The Spirit's mercy was apparent as the aura and the colors flickered and nearly extinguished. The sprigs of holly floating above his head dropped some berries that now dried up from their former bright red, into withered brown remnants, and they fell from their leaves. The Spirit waved his arms in the air and released the bondage of Steed.

Absalom Steed fell to his knees, tears rained down his cheeks. He held his arms and hands out at the scene in front of him, and cried out, "Don't leave her!

Don't! You loved her then and still love her now! Please, don't do this! Stop and think!"

The present-day Absalom Steed lowered his head to his chest and shook his head back and forth.

His voice came out as a whisper, "We could have had such a wonderful life together."

"He cannot hear you, Mr. Steed. This is merely a vision. Just a vision of what was, and it is unchangeable."

The present-day Absalom Steed sobbed as they watched while his younger self angrily took the ring from Betty Anne Lawton. He turned and looked at her and had the ultimate words that pierced the air and the present Absalom Steed's soul.

"I never want to see you ever again."

With those words, the younger Steed opened the door to the room and stepped out to join his father.

The present, Mr. Absalom Steed, hung his head and cried as the Spirit of Christmas gently reached out and took Steed's hand, and in a flash, they were spinning around in the air once more.

WHEN THEY STOPPED SPINNING and landed, they stood just inside the front doorway of a modest home. It was neat, clean, and furnished with some standard décor. It was not opulent, but it was not downtrodden, either. Middle-class. A Christmas tree stood in the corner of the living room, its lights happily glowed and broadcasted warmth and some Christmas presents sat neatly tucked underneath the tree. There were some crackling logs in a brick fireplace; a fireplace with a wide hearth that had additional wood stacked on one side, and a Christmas decoration of a sled with reindeer hitched to it on the opposite side. On a table at the end of the room, a table radio softly played Christmas music. A middle-aged man sat cross-legged on a sofa near the Christmas tree and the fire. He wore a plaid flannel shirt and a pair of workman's pants. They were the type of pants with many pockets, as are handy to carry tools with when working on a job. His hands were strong, his husky face deeply lined with worry. He sipped a generous pour of whiskey in a short tumbler glass, taking gentle sips as he stared into the fire.

Mr. Steed slowly recovered from his anguish of the previous vision.

He observed the new vision and commented, "We are on the east side of the city. Are we not, Spirit?"

"Perceptive, Mr. Steed. We are."

"Yes, these styles of homes are very prevalent here. I know them well. Not well to do. Not poor. Solidly middle-class. They build all these homes with honor and fortitude. I know that man," Absalom Steed told the Spirit. "That is Thomas Worrall. He owns the company that has the service and maintenance contract for the machinery at my factory." Steed's eyes wandered around the home and he commented, "Not a bad place he has here. I guess he does rather well."

The Spirit of Christmas looked at Steed and spoke in his melodious voice just a few words, "Correction. He used to."

"What do you mean, he used to, Spirit?" Steed questioned the words.

"Have you already forgotten your own actions, so soon, Mr. Steed? You terminated his company's services yesterday, Mr. Steed. Therefore, he used to have the service and maintenance agreement for your factory's machinery and he used to do rather well."

Despite all that they had seen and witnessed and the lessons learned so far, Steed's obstinate self and meanness lingered. It would not leave so easily. Absalom Steed's meanness had resilience.

"Well, it is Worrall's own fault and the fault of that softie, Wesley Shook, to allow it to linger so long. Worrall did not fulfill his obligations of the service agreement, and I have a business to run. After all, business is paramount and production rules my world."

The Spirit of Christmas put his fingers to his lips, and said, "Oh yes! You and your silly production nonsense, Mr. Steed. My goodness! Please, be quiet and hush, Mr. Steed. Watch and learn. There are excellent reasons as to why he did not arrive in a timely manner to repair your beloved machine."

The Spirit pointed at the scene in front of them and Steed sensed there was more to learn. He nodded and focused on what the vision showed them. A young woman appeared in the doorway between the living room and the kitchen of the home. She stood directly in front of Absalom Steed and the Spirit while holding a mug of coffee in her hand. The resemblance between the man on the sofa and the young woman was easy to see. Father and daughter.

Thomas Worrall looked up and smiled at the young woman.

He set his glass of whiskey on a coaster decorated with the artwork of a Christmas wreath that sat on an end table next to the sofa.

Thomas Worrall carefully studied the young woman's face and asked, "How is she doing now?"

He patted the sofa next to him to indicate that she should come and sit with him. The young woman smiled and made her way to her father's side.

When she sat next to her father on the sofa, she explained to him, "She is sleeping now. She is very comfortable. I gave her the pain medication. She wanted the radio next to the bed turned on with the Christmas music, and I tuned it to radio station WPAT and set the volume for her. The program is lovely, The Spirit of Christmas. It is very gentle and peaceful."

Thomas Worrall pointed at the radio on the table and smiled as he agreed, "It is. I have it playing here, too. I am so thankful that your mother is resting." He leaned in and put his arm around his daughter as she tucked into her father's body and rested her head upon his shoulder. Mr. Worrall's daughter lifted the coffee mug and took a sip.

"Your mother loves Christmas so much. I hope she can rest tonight and enjoy the day tomorrow. Just a little. I bought her a special gift."

With those words, the aura glowed brighter above the Spirit of Christmas and some red berries sprouted onto the holly leaves, filling the previously barren locations voided by the withered berries.

"I am so sorry, Dad, that I could not make it home until now. I heard about the loss of the Steed contract. Something about not making it in time to service a special machine."

Thomas Worrall nodded, and he picked up the whiskey glass from the end table, took a sip, and then placed it down on the coaster. He stared into the fire for a few seconds and did not immediately respond to his daughter's comments.

After some pensive thought, Mr. Worrall said, "No, sorry, ever, my lovely and precious daughter. You are doing all that you can. Your education is important, you are working part time, and we all do what we can. If only we had better healthcare insurance or the money to pay to get your mother into New

York City. I mean, the hospitals here in Paterson are good and they are doing all they can, but if we could afford a transplant, your mother might have a chance. The doctors say her blood type is working against us, too. To find a suitable donor and a kidney that her body won't reject is another huge obstacle. The doctor says there are more advanced methods available but they are so costly and we are almost broke now, anyway. Even with the insurance."

Absalom Steed narrowed his eyes at the scene, his ears twitched with the words of the vision, and upon hearing the conversation, Steed turned to the Spirit of Christmas and asked, "Spirit, tell me and reinforce what I recall. Mr. Shook told me that Mrs. Worrall is very ill with kidney disease. Specifically, are her both of her kidneys now failing?"

"Yes. Her dialysis sustains her, but her body grows weaker and weaker. It has now reached the critical stage. It is a disease you know all too well, Mr. Steed. All too well."

"I do. I certainly do," Steed agreed. "Mr. Worrall mentioned her blood type as being an obstacle. Spirit, I know you are all knowing. What is Mrs. Worrall's blood type?

"Blood type O, Mr. Steed. The same as your grandmother, your aunt, your mother and . . . you. She needs an O donor. Not an impossible situation, but not the best situation, Mr. Steed."

Steed nodded and rubbed at his chin. It was obvious that Steed was deep in thought.

He pointed at the vision and asked, "What are the young daughter's studies in, kind Spirit?"

"Social worker's duties. She desires to help those in need, Mr. Steed."

Steed sighed deeply and focused again on the vision as Thomas Worrall spoke, "Absalom Steed is a very important man. A man who runs a very successful production business. He is demanding, unreasonable, mean, obstinate, and difficult, but he is correct in terminating our agreement. I did not fulfill the terms and business is business. Your mother is more important than any contract is. I will find another one. We will make it without the Steed contract. Somehow, some way."

"But it is the bulk of our yearly business, Dad. How will the company survive?"

"It is. No question that it is, but we will work hard, we will pray and we will make it somehow. You will stay in school, graduate, your mother will beat this awful disease and we will make it. We need to stay positive and persevere."

Absalom Steed sighed again and mumbled, "Mr. Worrall's faith is strong, and he is a brave man. A genuine man. He chose his wife's health and well-being over his business. That was the correct choice. I was correct according to the terms of the agreement, but not correct in terms of humanity. I see now, the error of my actions and the consequences thereof them kind Spirit. I know you can see next Christmas and all the celebrations of the past, present, and the future. What is to become of Mrs. Worrall?"

"It is not pleasant, Mr. Steed. Next Christmas there will no presents under the Christmas tree for her. In fact, there is no Christmas tree or holiday celebration of any kind. There is sorrow and there is mourning. Mrs. Worrall will die. Mr. Worrall will sell the house and most of his possessions. His business will fail, the daughter will abandon school, and Mr. Worrall will be destitute. Nevertheless, what of it, Mr. Steed? Exactly what part of this situation is your problem?"

Absalom Steed hung his head and sobbed. He shook his head slowly back and forth in a reflection of his inner sorrow at the reality of the Spirit's prediction and in recognition of his horrible words and wretched behavior. When the Spirit held out his hand, Steed quietly and without hesitation accepted it, and off they were in a bright flash of red, green, and blue lights while they were off spinning to the next adventure.

WHEN THEY STOPPED SPINNING and landed, they stood just inside the front doorway of a tiny home. An old Cape Cod home, on a seedier side of the city. The home was on the north side of Paterson, near the Haledon Borough border. It was small and compact, with a tiny living room, a kitchen, and what you might perceive to be a dining nook on the first floor, a staircase with bedrooms and a bathroom upstairs. Maybe the home totaled eight-hundred square feet at the most.

There was a tiny Christmas tree on a table stand in the corner of the living room, with a smattering of gifts underneath the tree, a plastic Christmas wreath hung on the front door, a few assorted Christmas lights blinked in the front window facing the street and a mistletoe ball hung from between the archway of the kitchen to the living room. Despite its tiny size, the home was clean and neat and it smelled heavenly. There was some baking going on in the kitchen oven, and the aroma of a cake or bread or something delicious wafted through the home. A table radio, once more played Christmas music, tuned to what seemed as if it were the omnipresent Christmas radio program offered by the local radio station, WPAT.

The Spirit of Christmas was all around Mr. Absalom Steed in so many ways.

Steed pointed at the radio and smiled as his words were his first attempt at humor in what seemed as if it were ten lifetimes, "Ha! That radio program follows us all around. It is very popular. Everywhere we go. No infernal Christmas music here. Only beautiful music, Spirit."

The Spirit of Christmas was very pleased with Steed's actions and words, and he smiled widely.

"I will venture a guess here, kind Spirit. Based upon the pictures on the wall here, and some other telltale signs—that we are in the home of my manager, Mr. Wesley Shook?"

The Spirit nodded, smiled, and bowed in affirmation as the words came out of his mouth even more melodious and gentler than ever before, "We are," the Spirit held his arms outstretched and the aura of colors grew brighter and brighter and the holly sprung forth with more red berries until it overflowed with berries.

Steed watched in awe and he pointed at the display and commented while he did so, "Your aura ebbs and flows with the visions, with the themes of the various scenes that we witness and the holly grows many berries. It is beautiful, and it fascinates me, but I understand it now. It is a correlation between the amounts of Christmas cheer that we witness. When the visions are sad and emotional, your spirit drops, and the colors fade and the holly and the berries wither and die away. When the scenes and people we witness are full of Christmas happiness, your aura of lights grows in intensity of colors and the holly springs forth in growth and in an abundance of the berries."

"Correct, Mr. Steed. After all, I am the Spirit of Christmas. Look upon this scene! See how Mr. Shook understands the meaning of Christmas. Despite his meager circumstances, he and his family persevere!"

The Spirit pointed. Absalom nodded, and they directed their attention to the scene unfolding before them.

The front door to the small home flew open and three children dashed into the home. Their exuberance overflowed with energy and excitement. First, there was a tall, lean young girl; a girl who appeared to be the oldest of the children, as she seemed to be a young teen of thirteen or fourteen years of age. Another boy, who appeared to be a few years younger than the girl was, made a gleeful appearance behind his sister, and the boy's face was red from the cold and full of excitement and Christmas joy. Then, squeezing through the doorway behind his siblings, there was a small boy of perhaps nine to ten years of age, and finally, following behind the children, Mr. Wesley Shook appeared. His roly-poly wobble was all too familiar to Absalom Steed, as was his round face and beaming smile. They removed their overcoats and hats, stomped the snow off their boots, and left them on a floor mat near the front door. When they removed the heavier garb, Steed and the Spirit could see that all the family wore what might be their best clothes. Wesley Shook wore a jacket and a tie, the young girl wore a tidy dress, and the boys wore jackets and ties, too. The clothes were a little threadbare and certainly not very fancy. In fact, they looked as if they were second-hand clothes, but they looked clean and neat and refreshed.

Steed turned to the Spirit and commented, "My, goodness. Mr. Shook has a large family. I never knew that he had three children. All of these people in such a tiny home. And to raise them on his salary, my, it seems daunting."

The Spirit of Christmas rolled his eyes in his head and spoke in a voice less melodious than it previously was, "There is so much that you do not know, Absalom Steed. Because your bitterness has made you blind to aspects of life that do not profit you or make you money or increase your wealth. Daunting, Mr. Steed. Ha! Yes, you will learn exactly how daunting it is. Why are you surprised? After all, you gave him such a generous salary increase . . . how many years ago and how much was your overflowing generosity, Mr. Steed?"

Steed folded his arms across his chest and screwed his mouth up like a corkscrew as the recollection caused him a great deal of discomfort.

His words were a haphazard mumble of shame, "A nickel raise. Eight years ago, Spirit."

"Tsk, tsk, so generous, Mr. Steed. How could you ever afford such an enormous increase in wages to your loyal right-hand person? Let's see, Wesley Shook's keenness and sharp-eyes caught a ten-thousand-dollar error and you rewarded him with a nickel per hour raise. I dare to say that was a shrewd deal on your part and quite the return on your investment!"

"Hrrmmmpppp," Steed mumbled harshly and in a low growl as they redirected their attention to the vision.

"We are home, Mom! We are home!"

The children screamed in unison as they tore into the kitchen.

"Is that bread I smell baking? It smells glorious!" Wesley Shook said as he tilted his little round nose in the air to sample the scent.

The response came from the kitchen.

"It is. For Christmas dinner tomorrow. I also baked some extra loaves. I baked some raisin bread too. I thought that we could give them away at church for gifts and bring some to the Worrall's home. Pay them a Christmas Day visit and wish them blessings. I also stuffed the turkey and prepared it for the feast and celebration tomorrow. I hope an eight-pound turkey is enough for us all. However, the price was so high this year. I put extra stuffing in there and there is the bread and extra vegetables too! And of course, I have my famous homemade apple and mince pies!"

Steed mumbled and commented, "An eight-pound bird for all these people? My goodness! That is not enough food for such a large family. Yet they are giving away food as gifts? That seems as if it is not the wisest use of what appears to be limited funds available for a holiday celebration. They need to recheck their budget allocations and figures."

The Spirit did not answer or comment, but he continued to point at the scene of the vision in front of them.

The voice was a woman's voice, and it was sweet, gentle, and warm. In the distance of the kitchen there was an unusual noise, almost as if it was a sound of metal striking upon metal, and suddenly in the doorway between the rooms, a wheelchair appeared with a middle-aged woman sitting in it. Her face glowed with a genuine warmth; smiling and beautiful with a fair complexion, a dance of freckles across her nose and upper cheeks and neatly prepared black hair worn with a ponytail tucked behind her head. The resemblance of the children to their parents was keen.

Her round eyes were clear but had some whispers of sadness to them and as she propelled the wheelchair, she did so with some winces of pain and grimaces on her mouth. She stopped the chair under the mistletoe as she pointed up and smiled at it.

"Well, how convenient, I stopped under the mistletoe."

The children laughed and dashed over, and one-by-one gave their mother a hug and a kiss on the cheek. When the children finished expressing their love, Wesley Shook playfully glided in, hugged his wife, and gave her a long kiss on her lips.

Wesley Shook stood up, performed a comical shake and wiggle on his little round body and as the children laughed, their father said, "What a kiss! What a woman! She makes me shake all over!"

"I see their love is very deep, Spirit. The entire family is very close. It is easy to see this. Please tell me, because until now, I did not know that Mrs. Shook required the use of a wheelchair. What happened?"

The Spirit shook his head in dismay at the words and explained, "Are you that oblivious to humanity, Mr. Steed? You ignore the world around you unless it involves work, production, or has monetary value attached to it! Do you recall about three years ago? An accident . . . an errant fall . . . Mr. Shook using his vacation days up when his wife was in the hospital and when he ran out of time, you docked his paycheck for the missing time at work. Well, Mrs. Shook suffered a spinal injury in the accident and since then, well, here she is. She requires a specialized operation and extensive physical therapy and recovery. Then, perhaps, there is a chance at mobility. Perhaps. However, with your generous salary and overflowing medical benefits that barely pay for a hangnail and boast a range of deductibles that are to the moon and back, I am afraid that serious operations are out of the question."

Steed's anguish was deep at the words and with the realization of the pain that he contributed to, as well as his horrible treatment of, his loyal manager.

While he pondered his dismay, Steed looked around the home and commented, "I am aware of the layouts of these types of homes. They are quite common here in this section of the old city. There is only one bathroom upstairs and all the bedrooms are on the second floor." Steed then asked, "How does she navigate the stairs? I see that there is no motorized lift system installed on the staircase."

"Wesley Shook carries her. Yes, his love is deep, Mr. Steed. Very deep. His loyalty and kindness overflows. Look!"

"How was the Christmas Eve service at the church?" Mrs. Shook asked as the children dashed into the living room to sneak peeks at the gifts underneath the tree and try to guess as to what wonder they might bring. There were, at the most, seven or eight gifts in total that sat waiting there. Perhaps there were one or two gifts for each individual and the remaining gifts were for sharing amongst the family.

"It was a marvelous service. Singing Silent Night during the candlelight part of the service is so peaceful and joyful. How I hope you can attend next year's Christmas Eve service. Tonight, was so snowy and icy, and I understand your apprehension . . . but next year . . . next year, we will somehow find the money for your operation and you will be there with us! I prayed hard for that tonight, my dear," Wesley Shook explained as he passionately broadcasted the hope of his prayers.

"Thank you, my love. I hope so too."

"And I prayed very hard for Mr. Steed."

"Steed?" Mrs. Shook mumbled as her mouth turned down and her demeanor changed at the mention of the name of Absalom Steed.

"Why, Wesley? Why, Mr. Steed? After his evil behavior today and his meanness toward you and the termination of poor Mr. Worrall's company. The man should be ashamed at his horrible behavior and his evil words! Every day he just adds another layer of misery to his miserable life and drags everyone around him into his misery. His wealth means nothing and all he worries about is adding to it. Where will he ever spend such a grand amount of money? My goodness, he is an awful, awful man. Such shameful and obstinate behavior! At Christmas nonetheless! Why there has never been a meaner, more contemptible, hard-hearted, sour, and bitter man than Absalom Steed is!"

"Oh, my dear, no! We need to pray always. I prayed that Mr. Steed would have an awakening, an intervention for his good. I believe deep down that he is a good man. That life twisted and turned him to his bitter ways, but that he hides God's love deep within his heart. I prayed for the spirit of Christmas to fill his soul this year and renew his purpose in his life. I did, my dear. I did. I never prayed harder or more thoughtfully."

"Oh, my dear, Wesley. Never has there been a kinder man than you are, my love. I love you dearly. I am such a lucky woman to have such a man for my husband!"

"I love you too, my dear. Always and forever. And the children, and this world, and Christmas, and all it means to us! Merry Christmas to all! We are all greatly blessed!"

Wesley Shook held his arms out and his children rushed to his side and jumped up and down in celebration.

The Spirit of Christmas laughed uproariously at the joy of the scene, and he waved his arms frantically in the air toward where the Shook family stood. As he did so, the holly floating above his head sprouted even more berries until they overflowed the branches and they broke off from the branches and rolled onto the floor and towards the people in the vision. The berries jumped in the air and surrounded the family in a circle that changed into the same magical colors of the Christmas aura that surrounded the Spirit, and they popped and exploded as if they were starbursts of colors. Steed was awestruck at the amazing display of beautiful colors and at the power of the Spirit of Christmas.

The family began to sing along to the music playing on the radio, "God rest ye merry gentlemen! Let nothing you dismay. . .."

As the colors and the power of the aura faded away, Absalom Steed's eyes filled with tears and they streamed down his cheeks as if they were rivers emptying the despair from Steed's soul. Replacing the despair, Steed's soul absorbed hope, joy, and peace from the Spirit of Christmas. The pointy features permanently left his face, his ears did not twitch, and his face grew fuller. It gained a soft red glow of color in his cheeks, and his face reflected joy and kindness.

Steed's memories overflowed; he spoke gently, solemnly, and he spoke with a new purpose and a revelation, "My father's words, generous Spirit of Christmas. I can somehow recall and repeat them verbatim. Perhaps, that is your influence on my mind. Anyway, my father told me as he burned in rims of fire, 'When you think that you have lost everything, Christmas, and the blessed Savior, arrives to save us all. That is the message! The purpose. The joy and the hope. Sadly, I chose to turn away from the message and my fate is what it is. Forever sealed to doom. You still have a chance! A chance at the joy and a chance to share the hope. There was an intervention of some sort. Of what I am not sure, but an intervention on your behalf and there is an allowance for me to be here, to warn you, to allow you to see me and be a witness to my terrible fate, to steer you so that you have a chance at escaping the power of Satan.'"

Steed turned to the Spirit and studied the aura and the colors and Steed's eyes were round and wide, "It was the prayers of Wesley Shook. The prayers invoked the intervention. Mr. Wesley Shook saved me from Satan's power!"

"Yes, it was Mr. Shook's prayers that invoked the intervention, Mr. Steed. The power of prayer is unfathomable. Mrs. Shook's proclamation is profoundly correct and true. Because never has there been a kinder man than Mr. Wesley Shook is."

"I see! I see. Oh, kind Spirit I need to thank you, thank my dear father, and Mr. Shook, and all the powers of Heaven and of Earth, the moon, and the stars. I can do much good in this world and help Wesley Shook and his struggling family and find a way for Mrs. Shook to walk again. I must not forget the Worrall family! Mrs. Worrall! Oh my! She will live. By the grace of God and the love of Christmas, she will live! This time, we will beat that awful disease. This time we will win!" Steed wiped at his tears and he smiled at the Spirit, who laughed and smiled at the joy, too.

"Remember, Mr. Steed, it is not what you gained in life but what you sought that counts the most."

"I will seek to do well! I am a very wealthy man, you know, Spirit. I can do much good in this world and still have mountains of money left over!"

"I know, Mr. Steed. Now, you are wealthy in much more than mortal money. You are wealthy in love and the spirit of Christmas, too."

"Of course, you know that I am very wealthy. You know everything! I assure you that I am a different man! The power of these lessons will not leave me. I now feel the spirit of Christmas fill my heart and my soul. This has revived me! It is as if I am drunk on wine!"

Steed jumped up, clicked his heels together, turned, and joined in singing the rest of the song with the Shook family and the melodious golden voice of the Spirit of Christmas.

"I know the words! I do! I do recall them. Every verse," Absalom Steed assured the Spirit as he sang along with joy at the very top of his lungs. Mr. Steed had a marvelous singing voice!

When the song ended, the vision grew dim, and the voices faded away.

The Spirit looked at Mr. Steed and said, "Our time grows very short, Mr. Steed. We need to make haste. You will need a plan to contribute to this weary world. One more vision that you must see, Mr. Steed, before we part. One more vision."

The Spirit of Christmas gently reached out and took Steed's hand, and in a flash, they were spinning around in the air once more.

Chapter Five
Redemption

MR. ABSALOM WICKHAM Steed opened his eyes when he felt his feet touch the ground. When he did so, he found that he stood in ankle deep snow and, for the first time in all his journeys with the Spirit of Christmas, he felt the influence of the ice, snow, and cold. In fact, it was the first time in forever that he could recall that he felt the influence of any type of weather on his person. He shivered and wrapped his bathrobe around his body (he was still in his bedclothes!) and lifted his bed slippers up and out of the snow as the cold infiltrated deep into his feet and ankles. Mr. Steed looked at the scene in front of him.

It was not a pleasant sight.

In front of them stood the Steed Lace Factory. Or what appeared to be the Steed Lace Factory. It certainly did not look as it did today, or last week, or at any time in its long and glorious history.

The factory was in ruins.

The once proud sign proclaiming "Steed Lace Factory" was virtually unreadable from weathering. The sign hung by one edge to the gutter of the roof. It was full of icicles and tears, tilting down to the ground, and was ready to fall to the ground to develop into rot and ruins. A fence surrounded the property; a fence strapped with signs sternly warning against trespassing. Some sections of the fence fell over and were broke and collapsed. One side of the roof fell into the building, the windows were missing and shattered and the snow piled up inside. Brown, dried wisps and stalks of weeds poked up through the snow and they were everywhere; alongside the building, in the parking lot, and inside the fence line, and the weeds rattled and shook in their frozen state as they fought the bitter winter winds.

"What is this, Spirit? I mean, is it the future? Is this the fate of my life's work? My family's heritage?"

"It is. We are here on Christmas Day in 2022. The future, Mr. Steed."

Steed looked around dumbfounded and his eyes scanned the state of his factory as well as the surrounding neighborhood. He pointed at the dye factory and the houses and the smaller buildings all around them on Cliff Street and on Belmont Avenue and beyond.

"And these businesses are gone, too. Everything is in ruins. In disrepair. Vacant. Abandoned. The few homes remaining here appear to be desolate and rundown beyond repairs. What has happened to these thriving businesses and my beloved Paterson, New Jersey? Was it a war? Were we attacked by some evil country and lost?"

The aura of the Spirit of Christmas grew so dim that Steed could hardly even see the colors of it, and the berries withered and fell into the snow. The Spirit looked so much older now. Lines of age covered his face and the Spirit of Christmas appeared weathered and cold and pale. His eyes told of the sadness and he looked upon Mr. Steed with worry as his words arrived without their usual singsong melody.

"It was worse than an attack from another nation with evil intentions. It was an attack from within. Greed, power, profit, control, evil corporate executives, and magnates and decision makers of big business in the United States and corrupt politicians looking for power and payoffs while lining their pockets with stocks and shares and bonus money. When they found they could make unfathomable profits with cheaper labor and cheaper goods, they allowed foreign countries to produce goods and ship them here. They destroyed manufacturing in America with inexpensive overseas labor and inferior quality goods that they could sell at high profits."

"I don't understand, Spirit. This is America. We built this great country with manufacturing, and this is the great Silk City of Paterson, New Jersey. Please explain more to me."

"Politicians made agreements for foreign trade that were foolish, aiming to favor cheaper goods and labor. They adjusted tariffs and taxes and rules and regulations in favor of overseas competition. Politicians could not see the vision through their blindness of corruption and payoffs, the labor unions would not budge on wages, and manufacturing collapsed when they could not compete with the foreign manufacturing and products. In many ways, your father was correct when he said the demands of the unions were unfair."

Steed lifted his eyes toward the factory and mumbled, "Father. My dear father. If only his bitterness did not allow him to die so tainted. Now the unions have no jobs for the workers at all. All these jobs gone, the workers, their families. What do they do?"

"They work at lower wage jobs. America is no longer a manufacturing leader. The majorities of the jobs are now retail and service jobs. Support jobs. Those do not pay the higher wages of manufacturing. American steel is gone, Bethlehem, Pennsylvania, is a ghost town, and Pittsburgh is no longer known for steel manufacturing. Cleveland Ohio is suffering greatly and they label the region the Rust Belt of América. And in New England, they shuttered the garment mills and shoe factories forever. Most automobiles are of foreign parts and origins. Gone too, are American-made televisions, radios, stereos, and electronic products of all types. Gone are American garments, shoes, clothes, plastics, metals, and now they manufacture virtually everything overseas. They lost all these jobs. All gone."

Steed shook his head and asked, "What of England? Did their manufacturing industries survive? We partnered with them. We ruled the free world. Manufacturing won the war! Surely, despite the price, the world values the quality of our products over cheaply made inferior goods!"

"No, Mr. Steed. It is the same fate there as here. Quality versus price. Price wins. Profit over quality. Profit wins. Your partner factories are gone too. I show you this vision so you can plan for the future. Survive and prosper, Mr. Steed. Adjust because this is unchangeable and inevitable. The greed, power, and avarice that you once felt in your heart overtake most of humankind in this horrible day and age!"

Absalom Steed stood in the snow and the ice and cold, and he looked at the future. He folded his arms across his chest and remained deep in thought. The Spirit of Christmas allowed him some time to linger here in the future because he knew of its purpose to do so.

Suddenly, Steed clapped his hands together and, with a rebirth of enthusiasm, Steed turned to the Spirit and said, "Thank you for showing me this situation, Spirit. I know what I must do. First, I will enlist the aid of Mr. Shook. He has a very good business mind, you know, Spirit. We will partner with good men and solid companies such as Worrall Machinery and Mr. Tompkins at Tompkin's Machinery. Surely, their skilled mechanics have great skills to repair many types of machines. Steed wealth can fund the visions, and we all can prosper and take good care of our present and future families. We will all retool together to branch out into different types of machines, perform skilled, high-quality repairs, of what at this point, I exactly do not know, but maybe vehicles, refrigeration equipment, heavy equipment, maybe more focus upon repair rather than manufacturing. Diversify our businesses. We will not fail, kind Spirit! Failure is not an option! I will revive the Steed Foundation and we will help poor families with charities and kindness, and build better hospitals and help our fellow residents of this great city and beyond! Reestablish the Steed mansion and repair it to its former glory and, by goodness, mark my words, you and I will host a Christmas Eve party there next Christmas to rival the best Steed parties of the past. Make my grandfather proud! One day, I will be long gone from this world, but the seeds of goodwill that we will plant right now will continue forever."

Upon hearing Mr. Steed's words, the Spirit of Christmas smiled widely and waved his hands in the air. The holly sprigs sprouted fresh growth, and the aura grew to its usual glory as the Spirit glowed in Christmas magic. His appearance restored to its magical holiday glow, and the Spirit grew younger and more vibrant than ever before in its appearance and actions.

The Spirit lifted a finger and said in a low voice, "I will be there. At the party, you know, Absalom. Only you will see me, though."

"Yes! And, will I see you? Please assure me of that fact dear, Spirit of Christmas. It makes me sad to think that our time together ends here and now."

"You will always see me and feel my presence at every Christmas and many days in between too. Forever. As a reminder, here, take some holly berries from my sprigs and slip them in the pocket of your robe as proof of our encounters and of your rebirth."

The Spirit of Christmas reached up over his head and plucked a few plump red berries from the sprigs and handed them off to Steed. Steed slipped them into his pocket as he listened to the words of the Spirit.

"If we live every day as if it was Christmas, we will always have joy in our hearts. I will never leave you, Mr. Absalom Wickham Steed. Now, it is time to go! Hold my hand. It is time for you to return to the present. To Christmas, and to all the joy and the peace it brings! Hurry now. There is much great work to do! Above all, wish everyone far and wide a merry Christmas!"

This time, when they went off spinning on their fantastic journey, Mr. Absalom Steed did not scream out in fear. Instead, he laughed the entire way and sang verses to various Christmas songs at the top of his lungs.

WHEN MR. ABSALOM WICKHAM Steed opened his eyes, he scanned his surroundings. He was in his bed, in his bedroom, and he was still wearing his bedclothes on his body. Through a calculated squint of his eyes, he could detect a faint amount of daylight glowing through the bedroom window. Of course, the radio blared away with Christmas music and Absalom Steed smiled when he heard it. He popped up from his pillow and the first question that he had was if, in fact, it was still Christmas Day. His mind wandered with a hundred thoughts, a million different thoughts . . . and two million questions!

"Mr. Shook said that this radio station played Christmas music uninterrupted until midnight on Christmas Day. I suspect the overnight snow has stopped because I see the hints of sunlight peeking at me through the curtains. It is just daybreak, the sun is coming up, the Christmas music is playing, and therefore . . . it must still be Christmas Day!"

Steed removed the lanyard with the key to the wall safe from around his neck and tucked it in the drawer of his end table. He then jumped up out of his bed and danced around in the dusty old bedroom. He did not know what to do with himself first!

He stopped dancing and stood in the middle of the bedroom and thought, 'Wait! Was this actually a dream? Was this all real?'

Then he remembered the berries and deep in his heart, he knew the truth, yet he sought confirmation. With a quick dash, he found the pocket on his robe and, and, and, yes! They were there.

"Of course, it was not a dream! Bless you Spirit of Christmas! Bless you, Wesley Shook and my grandfather and father and, well, bless everyone! I hope that your mission of kindness to me brings you some salvation, dear Father. I will pray unceasingly for mercy upon your soul. Merry Christmas world! I am not sure what to do first. I wonder what time it is right now?"

Absalom ran off to the clock next to his bed and peered in at the dial.

He shouted out to the walls of his bedroom, "Seven o'clock in the morning! Yes! Christmas Day! I will make the best use of every minute. Every second, every moment. I need an open butcher shop or a supermarket. I need to send a real turkey to Wesley Shook and his family! Yes, at least a twenty-five pounder! Minimum! Maybe a thirty-pounder! The biggest turkey in New Jersey. And, I need to buy and send toys and gifts and some desserts, and pies and wine and beer and whiskey and, well, joy! To Shook and to Mr. Worrall! To the world!"

Steed put his hand under his chin and thought. Then he mumbled aloud again, "Where will I find a business open for support of all of this merriment? It is Christmas Day. Most establishments do not open today."

He sat on the end of his bed and his eyes scanned the bedroom as a smile appeared on his face. Absalom Steed smiled an awful lot as of these last few hours.

He snapped his fingers and said, "Well, of course. I am Absalom Steed! Absalom Wickham Steed! I just need to make a few phone calls, to key contacts, such as Mr. Jacobs at Jacobs-Twenty-Nine Downtown Department Store and some others from our business circles and they will make allowances. I will pay handsomely and be more than happy to do so! Yes! Tomorrow, first thing in the morning, I will call my attorneys, raise them out of bed on the day after this glorious holiday, and request their services to begin to resurrect the Steed Foundation! I will pay them double and triple time for their efforts! And they will all think that I lost my mind and I will relish the thoughts of it!"

Steed ran to the window of his bedroom, grabbed ahold of the window handle, and tugged it open with newfound zeal and strength.

The years of dust and cobwebs scattered.

The snow lay glistening beneath the window. Pure, crisp, and shining like a million diamonds in the gathering sunlight. It was cold, very cold, and peace was all around. Absalom Steed admired and relished it all and he took a deep breath and took in Christmas.

"Merry Christmas to all!"

He shouted out the window, and it echoed down Preakness Avenue, all the way across the old city. To the far reaches of the Great Falls and down the Mill District, over to the downtown streets, and the Totowa Section and into Hillcrest and Crooks Avenue and to the east side, the north side and into river side.

Throughout the land.

"Hallelujah!"

Absalom Steed made his phone calls, made his connections, ordered his goods, and planned his day. He attended a Christmas Day worship service at his family's long-time church that had not seen him grace the rafters, nor the carpet, nor the pews, in many, many years, and he wrote a check and dropped it into the collection plate that caused a few eyeballs of the clergy to spin!

"A great deal of back payments, pastor," Steed cried. "A great many!"

He received communion and sang the hymns at the top of his lungs; he danced home in the snow and had a snowball fight with some local children. Mr. Absalom Steed helped another group of children to build a snowman in the park. The huge snowballs were much too heavy for the children to lift into place and Steed gladly assisted in the task. After assisting in the snowman construction, Steed took a spin on a downhill sled with the children! Steed gave away dollars and joy to the street beggars and to every homeless person that he could find along his way and took down their information to offer future help and perhaps even jobs at his factory and within his new visions for his future business ventures.

Why, Absalom Steed even found a Christmas tree lot still open, and he purchased a fresh Christmas tree, while giving the tree seller an extra one-hundred-dollar-bill for his time on the holiday and a dusty old bottle of wine from the Steed wine cellars. Steed set the tree up in the foyer of his grand mansion and decorated it with cherished old ornaments and strings of Christmas lights rescued from the depths of banishment in the basement of the mansion. He lit the tree up and cried tears of joy at the sight of the beauty of it. Absalom Steed enjoyed a great feast ordered up from a local restaurant that he paid handsomely for, and then some more extra dollars for preparing the meal on Christmas Day and with such short notice. He searched for his old violin and found it in an upstairs closet. Steed sat on a stool and relived his music lessons. After struggling with tunes for a few hours, his skills returned, and he happily played some Christmas music on his faithful, stringed companion.

Steed celebrated the day in grand fashion. He did not waste a single second of Christmas Day! Not a single second!

He also planned for the next day!

Oh, what plans he had too!

THE CLOCK IN THE MANAGEMENT office of the Steed Lace Factory struck eight in the morning and there was no sign of Mr. Wesley Shook. Then it struck half-past the hour and Absalom Steed cackled in delight and rubbed his hands together in glee.

"Perfect. Mr. Shook is late. He was supposed to be here at eight o'clock. On the other hand, he agreed to be here even earlier! This is perfect!"

The office door burst open at quarter to the nine-o'clock hour and Mr. Wesley Shook pushed through it, blustery, red-faced and his roly-poly walk even more roly-poly than usual. He tore off his overcoat and hat, stomped the snow off his boots and hung them on the coat hook, and, with nary a glance toward his boss, he dove into his chair, opened his ledger, and pretended to scan the numbers.

"Good morning, Mr. Shook. I thought we had an agreement as to your time to report to work today," Mr. Absalom Wickham Steed growled in his best offensive voice.

Wesley Shook dropped his pencil, and he paused in slight shock at the change in Steed's appearance. Mr. Shook blinked hard, once, then twice, then a third time. He rubbed at his eyes and refocused. After a long and careful study, Mr. Shook determined that it was indeed Absalom Steed in front of him. However, Mr. Steed was no longer pointy, his face had color in it and he was smiling. Mr. Shook might even venture out on a limb and say that Mr. Steed looked . . . happy.

After the shocking and careful study, Wesley Shook spoke, "We did, sir. I am very sorry, but yesterday was quite the holiday . . . sir. It was extra . . . joyful and unusual. I became lost in the joy."

Steed folded his arms across his chest and erased his smile and instead, he put on a pretended puzzled look and asked, "How so, Mr. Shook?"

Wesley Shook stood up from his desk and he explained, "Well, Mr. Steed, first off, a local butcher shop, Aldon's Market from downtown Paterson, knocked on our front door and delivered the largest turkey that we have ever seen in our lives from an unknown donor. Thirty-one pounds! I dare say it took many hours to cook it, but there was never such a bird. We have leftovers forever! And there were baskets of fruit and there were breads, and pies, and candies and cakes, and then there were presents delivered to our home in waves of deliveries! I do mean with waves! One delivery after another."

Wesley Shook stopped speaking to wipe some tears away from his eyes. Once he recomposed, Mr. Shook spoke again.

"There were bottles of fine wine, and assorted pottery and bakeware for my wife, and a wonderful tea set for us to enjoy. There were hats, and coats, and scarves, and gloves, records, and a record player, three scooters, and a soccer ball and footballs, and hockey sticks and a badminton set. There were baseball bats and balls and mitts, three bicycles, a chess and checkers set, more board games, and you name it, and it arrived at our home. It was so wonderful. I do not know where it all came from, but it made for the greatest holiday. Then at eight-o'clock at night, yes, indeed, eight o'clock at night on Christmas Day, Mr. Steed, there was another knock at the door, and a deliveryman shocked us even more when he dropped off a brand-new, state-of-the-art, motorized wheelchair for my wife. Unfortunately, my dear wife must utilize a wheelchair. I might not have mentioned that before, Mr. Steed. The deliveryman explained how he will return after Christmas to install a motorized lift on our staircase to allow easy access for my wife to the upper portion of our home! And we do not know who sent us all of these marvelous things. Everything was anonymous. Yet, to say the least, it was shocking and marvelous and amazing and, of course, it was the greatest Christmas Day ever. I am still reeling and overcome with joy."

Wesley Shook poured out the details of his wonderful holiday and strange experience to Mr. Steed and after studying his face for a few seconds, Mr. Shook dared to ask, "Are you feeling okay today, Mr. Steed?"

"Never better, Mr. Shook. Never better in over twenty or so odd years. Why do you ask?"

"Well, sir, if I might say so, well, you look . . . happy. As in thrilled."

Seeing no immediate reaction from his boss to his observation, he slowly sat down in his chair and once more picked up his pencil and addressed the completion of his work.

Understandably, Mr. Shook was still very apprehensive.

"Sorry, sir," Wesley Shook mumbled.

"Shoooook!" Steed shouted.

Wesley Shook shot up out of his chair as if his pants were on fire and he stood quivering at attention next to his desk.

"Shook, as of right now, this very second, I relieve you of your duties as purchasing and production manager for the Steed Lace Factory."

Shook's face collapsed and Mr. Steed could not stand to see the pain so he quickly added, "And as of right now, this very second, today, I promote you to vice president in charge of, well, new business ventures, production, purchasing and anything else you want to add. In addition, there is a bonus of ten-thousand dollars in that envelope there in the tray with your name on it, and, well, your salary, well, I cannot think of the figures, so let's just triple it! Better yet, let's call it quad-tripled. Is that even a word? And I appoint you to the board of directors of the newly resurrected Steed Foundation. And you are the vice president of Steed Enterprises Unlimited. That is a new business venture we are creating. Together. These new assignments are all paid positions, of course. Above your regular salary! Over there in that box, there is Mr. Shaw's radio. I took some time, cleaned, and polished it. It is a unique and special radio. Please return it to Mr. Shaw as soon as possible. I will meet with him in person later today and offer my personal thanks and apologies, too. Right for now, we have much to do! Yes! Now, we have a big day ahead of us, Mr. Shook. A very big day! Please, make sure the loading dock supervisor of the day is aware of deliveries arriving today."

Wesley Shook held onto the edge of his desk in fear, and in shock and in a daze at the words and all that was happening right now. His head was spinning, and he was not sure what to make of it all.

"Promotions? Ten-thousand dollars? Deliveries, Mr. Steed? What is going on today? Ah, well, I don't know what to say, or to do, or . . . are you okay, Mr.

Steed? I know you never drink wine or whiskey or beer, but do I dare to ask if you wandered a little from your usual behavior and are inebriated? Deliveries?" A visibly shaken Mr. Shook stammered.

Steed stood up and smiled again with a smile so wide that Mr. Shook was sure that Steed's teeth would fall out of his mouth. Mr. Shook was sure that the world was ending.

Absalom Steed stood up and held his arms outstretched and proclaimed, "Ha! Ha! Ha! No, I am not half-in-the-bag, Mr. Shook. Sober, sober, sober. Perhaps, I am drunk with joy and Christmas spirit, but I have never felt better, Mr. Shook! Yes! Bonus money! Yes! Promotions! Yes, deliveries. New radios for all the crew! And no more work today. We have soda, wine, beer, cookies, snacks, and candies, and sandwiches and cakes arriving, and free turkeys and fresh hams for every employee! We have savings bonds for each and every employee and our vendors and contractors! There is a band on the way to play Christmas music all day long! All. Day. Long. I love Christmas music. Especially, that one song. God Rest Ye Merry Gentleman! Yes. Love it! Tell Billy to turn up the heat and join us! Fire that old boiler! Make us cozy and warm and snug as bugs in the rug. Merry Christmas, Mr. Shook!"

Mr. Shook backed up a little as his senses were wary and he thought for a second or two that Absalom Steed lost his mind.

Then Mr. Shook felt it too.

The Spirit of Christmas intervened.

Wesley Shook stood smiling, and he was aware of the change. The spirit, the soul, and the peace, hope, and the joy.

"Mr. Steed . . . did you send all of those glorious gifts and amazing food and drinks to my home?"

"No. Well, maybe sort of. Let's just say that the Spirit of Christmas did and leave it at that! Now, no more dawdling! We have a Christmas party to organize! Be to your duties, Mr. Shook! Ah, wait! Mr. Shook! Before you hustle off to tend to your additional duties, please call Mr. Thomas Worrall and restore his service contract. Send some other type of work to Tompkin's Machinery, too. Keep them all busy with work and contracts! Be creative, Mr. Shook. You have a brilliant business mind. We need to use it to our mutual advantages. Maybe, Billy has some repair needs on the boiler. And also, please make a note to call that radio station. What is it?"

Mr. Steed waved his hands in the air in the direction of Mr. Shook as he searched for the call letters of the station. It was as if he could not speak the words quickly enough. Steed spoke once again with continued enthusiasm.

"WPAT or whatever it is. Tell them we will sponsor the entire Christmas music program next year. Start to finish. I want to grab it before any other slick and smart companies dive in and sponsor it. I want to sponsor it with the Steed Lace Factory, with the Steed Foundation and the Steed Kidney Care Fund and Steed Enterprises Unlimited! Yes! Please, arrange it all now. No price is too high! I don't want to lose out on the opportunity to sponsor such a glorious program. Please, remind me, Mr. Shook. What is the name of that simply amazing radio program? The Spirit of Christmas?"

"That is correct, sir. Exactly. I will gladly take care of all these requests."

Mr. Steed waved his arms in the air as if he was mimicking a sign banner, and he laughed as he said, "I love it! Perfect! Sponsored by The Steed Foundation, Steed Lace Factory, Steed Kidney Care Fund, and Steed Enterprises Unlimited! Until now, you did not even realize that those organizations existed! Is that right, Mr. Shook?"

Wesley Shook laughed uproariously too and said, "Well, honestly, I do know of the Steed Lace Factory. For sure!"

Mr. Steed doubled over in laughter and pointed at Mr. Shook and said, "Of course you do, Mr. Shook! Of course. Now, Mr. Shook, please, hurry and attend to your tasks!"

"Yes, sir! My pleasure!" Mr. Shook exclaimed, then he smiled and then while he took a deep breath and stood in place, Mr. Shook closed his eyes, bowed his head, and prayed in silence. At first, Mr. Absalom Steed stood in silence, and then he, too, bowed his head and prayed. When both men finished praying and opened their eyes, they both observed that there were tears of joy running down their cheeks.

"Thank you, Mr. Steed from the bottom of my heart," Wesley Shook said as he rushed over with his hand outstretched to shake Steed's hand.

Steed, instead of shaking Mr. Shook's hand, warmly embraced Wesley Shook and while they hugged, Steed said, "Nonsense! No thanks required. It is I who needs to thank you, Wesley Shook. The power of prayer is unfathomable. I have recently resumed the practice once more in my own life after being wayward for too long. Merry Christmas, Wesley."

"Merry Christmas, Absalom."

MR. ABSALOM WICKHAM Steed did all that he said he would do, and then some more. The Steed Foundation, and the Steed Kidney Care Fund with the daughter of Mr. and Mrs. Thomas Worrall, Ms. Lilly Worrall at the helms, built hospital wings and donated specialized equipment. The foundation's charity efforts donated millions of dollars of money to inner-city families, provided food and shelter to those in need, and it helped the desperate and saved countless lives. Mr. Steed arranged for the best medical care available, he fronted the medical costs, and Mrs. Worrall beat her illness. Mr. Steed went on in his life with only one kidney and he was thrilled to do so! He was a direct match.

He arranged for the best medical care for Mrs. Shook and she walked again, albeit with a limp, and she attended Christmas Eve services in 1975 while walking into church under her own power! Mr. Worrall and Mr. Tompkins joined the Steed team, and everyone prospered. Mr. and Mrs. Wesley Shook and their family moved on from their tiny home and purchased a pleasant and spacious home in a quiet section of the city near the Totowa Borough border.

In the new business known as Steed Enterprises Unlimited, everyone earned a solid salary and enjoyed a worthwhile workplace.

Mr. Wesley John Shook, as predicted by Absalom Steed and noted, proved to have a keen business mind and when the world changed and the economy changed and the vision of the future proved true, Steed Enterprises Unlimited was well prepared for new lines of business and opportunities and they continued their nearly one-hundred-years of success. There were always free turkeys and hams at Christmastime for every employee, and never was there a better owner, boss, or person than Mr. Absalom Steed was.

Mr. Steed restored the Steed mansion and property into a showplace of grandeur, and every year he hosted the Christmas Eve party of all Christmas Eve parties. Everyone who was anyone, and then some, attended! Mr. Steed entertained the guests with his amazing skills on the violin while playing Christmas tunes.

In fact, Mr. Steed even sought out, begged for forgiveness, and miraculously rekindled a lost love and finally, finally, married his love, Betty Anne Lawton (who never married) at the ripe, young age of fifty, and what a wonderful life they had together! It was true love. They became leaders in the old city and donated much, if not all, of their time to charitable causes and missions. His face was always happy; his eyes round, bright, and clear. Mr. Steed's ears no longer twitched in anger or surprise because his soul was content. Mr. Steed cut his pointy fingernails and always kept them round and perfectly manicured. He no longer stomped around when he walked; instead, he glided gently across the floors and ground as if he floated. His back was straight and true. When he walked about the world, he joyfully observed everything around him and always greeted anyone he met along the way with a pleasant gesture and extra-extended warmth of kindness.

Absalom Steed never shared any details of his encounters, nor any of the visions, and some people who knew him before and after that fateful Christmas in 1974 marveled at the change in him, while others mocked him and chuckled. Steed did not care. It was because he knew the truth. He knew joy; he knew hope and, above all, he knew the Spirit of Christmas.

Mr. Absalom Steed, in his pocket, always carried around some ripe red holly berries as a reminder of his journey from despair to joy.

Berries that despite their age, never withered or lost their color.

Let it be a goal for all of us within our own lives and be a lesson to one and all, and everyone, everywhere. Never lose our color or wither.

Hallelujah!

THE END

There we go. Done!

I neatly tuck the last of the Christmas decorations away in their boxes. The tree, the lights, the ornaments, the wreath, and even the mistletoe.

The plastic version of mistletoe with the bell on the end of the red ribbon. It only cost me four dollars, and I must say that it was a wonderful bargain.

No one kissed me underneath the mistletoe this year. Nor last year, or countless years before this one. That is how it goes these days. Regardless of the lack of kisses, I milked a bit of joy from Christmas this year, as I do every year, and now it is time to move onto a new year and all the challenges ahead.

It seems so tragic to pack the holiday away in dusty old boxes, only to resurrect it all again in eleven months or thereabouts. It is indeed, an awful error to forget the beauty of the lights and the decorations or the glorious music that we only listen to a month out of the year, or to forget how we lose our hearts in lights all aglow and we no longer hear the message of Christmas. Instead, Christmas needs to remain in our hearts every day. To pack it away is a huge mistake.

In fact, it is a tragedy.

Christmas needs to remain close to us continuously. Yes! Continuously! No matter what your religious or your spiritual beliefs are, or other worldly beliefs are, Christmas certainly deserves not to go away at all. Certainly not to reduced remnants hidden away in boxes, banished to hide within spider-laden corners of our garages, basements, or attics. It is too glorious for that fate. Let us proclaim Christmas every day. Shout the message out loud and clear and for everyone to hear!

I have it now. I know what to do. I dig around, find that same plastic mistletoe ball, and pluck it from the confines of the storage box. The little bell rings as I hustle down the staircase and re-hang it on the hook over the doorway that I removed it from an hour or two earlier. I happily stare at it while it merrily hangs upon the hook. I stand under it and I ring the little bell.

The bell hanging on the end of the red ribbon.

Did I mention that it only cost me four dollars? A wonderful bargain for the joy that it brings to me! I might have mentioned that several times, dear reader. Please forgive me for doing so.

I ring the bell once more.

I feel a tear rim my eye.

The little bell rings, but no one arrives to kiss me, or hug me, or love on me, but that does not matter. In rethinking the mission of the mistletoe, perhaps we put too much pressure on the poor mistletoe.

Expected a little too much.

Perhaps the mistletoe is a metaphor for our own lives. We expect many things and feel let down when they do not happen or we fail in our perception of success and the endless pursuit of happiness. We need to toss away the material things and aspects of life and focus on the simpler things in life and not the grandiose things. Reel in our wanderings and focus our energies upon the incredible world that surrounds us. Yes, in giving it some thought, summoning love at the ring of the bell while standing underneath it and warding off evil is not the actual mission and the purpose of the mistletoe. No, no, no. It is so much more than that, my dear reader. I think the mission is to remind us that love exists in this weary world.

Along with peace, joy, and hope, too.

I think that I will keep this decoration here all year long. Because it is not the fact that no one arrives to love on me when I ring the bell and stand underneath it that matters, it is the fact that I know that I have love in my heart. Love is the source of my tear, not sorrow.

Love.

And that dear reader is the message of Christmas. Mr. Dickens used his character of Ebenezer Scrooge to show that even the worst of us, the vilest, and the most hardened of hearts, possess love. We just need a reminder.

A reminder that, despite our flaws, our sins, our humanness, our shortcomings, and our meagerness—we all have love in our hearts.

Ah yes, Christmas! Glorious, wonderful, magical, loving, blessed, colorful, remarkable, joyous, and blessed Christmas.

Excessive commas and all. I might have missed one or two. Unusual punctuation was good enough for Mr. Dickens; therefore, it is good enough for me, too.

Please, I beg that you forgive me.
I have a bell to ring.
Please, a happy Christmas to all.

. . . .

Commentary

A Christmas Carol

Mr. Charles Dickens

Mr. Paul John Hausleben

. . . .

IN MY WORK AND EFFORTS in, and of, writing musical reviews, part of the work that I did for God Bless the Keg Publishing LLC and others was to rank music records, artists, and various songs and tidbits. I very much enjoy ranking various things and items; I think many people do too. In fact, there are entire websites devoted to the ranking and rating of most anything and everything that you can ever conceive of! One of my favorites is the ratings for the best of the best of frozen pizzas!

Anyway, it is great fun and quite entertaining too. Deeper into this book, we will have some fun with lists and ratings. I love lists!

When we ranked and rated music, I always used a five to one scale of ranking. Five being great and one being superlative in every aspect. I felt anything beyond five was too subjective and too open. The five best selections are the five best of the best. It makes it very narrow, indeed.

In rating the five best stories ever written or books, or novels, or novelettes or whatever, from whatever genre that I can pick from, *A Christmas Carol* by Mr. Charles Dickens is my number one book, story or whatever. Hands down. There you go.

Cards are all face-up now.

Okay, why Paul?

There are so many magnificent pieces of literature from the minds and pens and creativity of Shakespeare, Tolstoy, Hugo, Michener, Chandler, and Sir Arthur Conan Doyle . . . you know them all. You love Raymond Chandler! Paulie, c'mon, Philip Marlowe, the ultimate tortured soul! You have Homicide Detective Lyle Odell as a character and Chandler had Marlowe! Admittedly, I do love the work of Chandler, however; Mr. Dickens is without peers.

Dear reader, together, let's jump into the book and see where it leads us. We can study and dissect some of the hidden nuances and magic of *A Christmas Carol*.

A CHRISTMAS CAROL is remarkably simple, yet deeply complex. On the surface, it is about an evil man who changes his ways, but within the maze of words and storylines, it is much more than a story of repentance. It is truly about the triumph of good over dark powers that invades our lives and pervades our societies.

I think every generation thinks that their own lifetimes see and experience the evilest, and I am sure that England in the lifetime of Mr. Dickens suffered from great despair and layers of corruption. Just as our world does now.

A Christmas Carol is about those who have and those who have not. That same timeless struggle of the rich versus the poor. It is timeless, as those struggles still exist and they have for as long as humankind has existed. Sadly, perhaps they always will.

Through my coursework, I became fascinated by Dickens's use of subtle and obvious Biblical, Christian, and Gospel references in his masterpiece. He also took long walks, particularly at night, through the streets of London to formulate parts and pieces of the story and create characters, dialogue, and scenes in his mind. While I am in no way comparing myself to the genius of Mr. Dickens, I felt a writing kinship with him upon learning of these facts. I too, include many religious, Christian, and Biblical references in my work; hidden and obvious. I also am prone to taking long walks at night throughout the apartment complex where the PJH Writing Command Center is. While writing, PJH is also a notorious pacer of the floor of the PJH Writing Command Center. That old apartment, which we lovingly renamed, is the location that I lived when I wrote nearly all my material. While it is not the nicest place in the world, or the most elegant, it will always be a very special place for me.

I shared parts and pieces of my soul with that old apartment and its humdrum walls and floors. Humdrum walls and floors are remarkable inspiration.

Mr. Charles Dickens was born to Anglican parents. He worshipped not only in the official Church of England but also as a Baptist and a Unitarian. Yet in his time, day, and age, England and particularly London was a complex location for Christianity. Social matters were complex and Dickens developed a distaste for how the world treated the poor and destitute; particularly the conditions that affected children. His own observations of the social injustices, his own experiences as a young child, forced to work in a horrible inking factory when the courts sent his father to debtor's prison and his general observations of the state of affairs in his time, all combined to inspire the roots of the storyline. Those same conditions and observations also provided inspiration for many of the characters for *A Christmas Carol*. Dickens felt that churches could do so much more for the poor and unfortunate. These observations, experiences, and opinions of Charles Dickens all combine to become central themes in *A Christmas Carol*. Yet, despite his disputes with the formal church and their staunch doctrines and dogmas, Dickens was a Christian. In fact, he wrote a book for his children, based upon the Holy Gospels, *The Life of Our Lord*; published after his death.

To delve deeper into the complexity of *A Christmas Carol*, there are numerous Biblical references throughout the book. The story abounds with religious symbolism.

Some references are obvious such as the name of the book itself. Taken from the young boys singing a carol on Christmas Eve while hoping for a few coins in return of their efforts. Scrooge chases them away from his office's front stoop as they sing "God Rest Ye Merry Gentleman." Just a lyric before the next line, which proclaims, the birth of our Lord and Savior. Another obvious reference is when Scrooge wants to drown out the bright light emitting from the Ghost Of Christmas Past with the ghost's own cap. The Ghost of Christmas Past confronts Scrooge by asking him why he wants to shut off the light.

**"Would you so soon put out, with worldly hands, the light I give?" The Ghost of Christmas Past asks. This is an obvious reference to Jesus and the proclamation of Jesus being the "Light of the World" casting out the darkness. We have a direct reference when Peter Cratchit reads from the Gospel of Mark about Jesus and the young child set amid the circle. We have Scrooge's nephew proclaiming God's blessing when he visits his uncle and Bob Cratchit in the office on Christmas Eve, as well as Tiny Tim with his classic proclamation of **"God bless us everyone!" Then we have the Ghost of Christmas Present travelling throughout the world and taking joy at the Christmas celebration scenes. The Ghost uses his torch to sprinkle a blessing and wave blessings of incense smoke, particularly at the home of Bob Cratchit and his family. The use of incense and the sprinkling of water for blessings is a common Christian religious practice.

Other Biblical and Christian refences are much deeper and not so obvious.

Aside from the struggles of the rich versus the poor and the unofficial commandment of Jesus to "Love thy neighbor," there are deep and complex references that Dickens utilized. We have Belle Scrooge's former finance, while breaking off the engagement and explaining to Scrooge that a golden love has replaced her. Worshipping of a golden idol. Ah yes! The downfall of so many in humankind!

We have the references and use of the number three. Throughout the Bible and God's teachings, the number three is of paramount importance. In *A Christmas Carol*, there are three ghosts, the city clock striking three o'clock, and there are three days of the storyline leading to Scrooge's conversion. Old Fezziwig had three daughters, and there are the three crooks who stole Scrooge's belongings after his death, and sold them to Old Joe. These examples and other references to the number three that Dickens sprinkles throughout the book, are hidden references to the Holy Trinity and the Biblical and Gospel use of the number three. They are a testimony to Charles Dickens's knowledge of religious teachings and of his Christianity.

Here are some Bible teachings to ponder in relation to the writing strategy of Charles Dickens for his masterpiece.

In the Bible, Peter's denial of Christ occurs, as predicted, with three denials before the evening. The period of Christ's death and resurrection occurs in a three-day period of Holy Thursday, Good Friday, and Holy Saturday, during the sacred Easter period. Jonah spends three days and nights in the belly of the fish. There are three gifts presented to the Christ child by the Magi. The number three abounds, and throughout *A Christmas Carol*, Mr. Dickens includes many,

many more religious references. I have touched on only a few here; I challenge a reader to dig deep and find them all!

It is fascinating.

To understand the power of the story, first, a reader needs to know and understand how awful a man that Ebenezer Scrooge was. He was not just a little grumpy and gruff! He is mean, as in very, very mean. Borderline evil.

Initially, in the opening words of the book, Dickens establishes from the powerful words and testimony of the narrator that Jacob Marley was dead. Dickens puts particularly heavy emphasis on that fact with the **"Dead as a doornail" statement and then uses a comparison to a coffin nail. A few paragraphs later, Dickens describes the layers of evil within Ebenezer Scrooge and that, dear reader, is where the heart of the story lies.

First, the author brilliantly describes Scrooge's physical appearance and then flows into his internal issues. In a few paragraphs of some of his most brilliant words in the manuscript, Dickens composes magic within this masterpiece while he sets the table for the reader to understand the true magnitude of Scrooge's discontent:

**"External heat and cold had little influence on Scrooge. No warmth could warm, no wintry weather chill him. No wind that blew was bitterer than he, no falling snow was more intent upon its purpose, no pelting rain less open to entreaty. Foul weather didn't know where to have him. The heaviest rain, and snow, and hail, and sleet, could boast of the advantage over him in only one respect. They often "came down" handsomely, and Scrooge never did."

The fact that Scrooge keeps his offices and his own home so cold is not only an empathic aspect that emphasizes to the readers, the miserly tendencies of Ebenezer Scrooge (being too cheap to buy coal) but it is a metaphoric reference to Dante's Inferno. Where Lucifer remains frozen in a block of ice in the center of Hell. So, is Scrooge as evil as is Lucifer is? My goodness!

Dickens then describes how no one speaks to Scrooge unless required too, how even the blind persons, led by their assistant dogs and companions, led their masters away from Scrooge when they crossed paths. Here, Dickens establishes that even seeing-eye dogs and non-humans recognize the depth of evil of Ebenezer Scrooge. Brilliant writing! Masterful!

Dear reader, please don't miss the power in brief descriptions and in small statements such as where Scrooge dines on Christmas Eve with his

**"Melancholy dinner in his usual melancholy tavern." He passes the special night, not in celebration, but in studying his banker book.

Each paragraph brings layers of genius in the words and in the pictures painted here by the author with his potent and detailed descriptions.

Another prevailing reason for my opinion that this is number one book and story of all-time on my list, and perhaps, the most compelling reason is the characters. If there is one thing that I share with Mr. Dickens. (Forgive my boldness in sharing anything with Mr. Dickens) in my own work is that I enjoy introducing multitudes of characters into my material. Major and minor characters of all sorts, and as Dickens does, I enjoy describing those same characters in intricate details. While other work by Mr. Dickens presents many endearing and unforgettable characters, (particularly, Oliver Twist) in my opinion, no other work left such a cast of characters on the pages as did *A Christmas Carol.*

Common thought is that Mr. Dickens lent upon many of the actual persons that he met in his own life to create the fictional casts of characters that he weaves into his stories. Of course, that is a natural method of inspiration for fiction writers. The longer that I live, and the more that I write, the more that I find myself doing the same thing. Scrooge leads the remarkable cast of characters. Of course, poor beleaguered Robert Cratchit and lame Tiny Tim, the various Ghosts and Jacob Marley, and so many other characters fall in line behind them. Notwithstanding any ratings thereof with the cast of characters because both the major and minor characters are just as powerful and as important as the lead characters, I have my favorites!

Mr. Fezziwig, in particular, is a powerful, important, and wonderful character. Unforgettable, because of his jovial and rollicking nature and the fact that his kindness and generosity lie in stark contrast to Scrooge's evil nature. While the story unfolds and we learn what caused Scrooge to become so covetous and tainted, we realize even more the importance of Old Fezziwig to the heart of the story. Even Dickens's description of the warehouse where Fezziwig directs young Scrooge and Mr. Wilkins to prepare for the Christmas party lies in stark contrast to Scrooge's own place of business and his living quarters too. Dickens expertly and strategically describes the warehouse in an important paragraph:

**"Every movable was packed off, as if it were dismissed from public life for evermore; the floor was swept and watered, the lamps were trimmed, fuel was heaped upon the fire; and the warehouse was as snug, and warm, and dry, and bright a ball-room, as you would desire to see upon a winter's night."

Unlike where he apprenticed, Scrooge's place of business is dirty, dark, cold, and miserable, as is his living quarters, which he apparently inherited when Jacob Marley passed, since Dickens relates how the home used to be Marley's home. The author describes the area where poor Robert Cratchit labors as **"The Tank." How awful a place!

The comparison is on purpose and reinforces the depth of Scrooge's despair.

The beauty of the story and magnificence of the words composed by the pen of the author is apparent as the reader progresses in their reading.

Deeper into the story, when the Ghost of Christmas Past presents a powerful and somewhat cynical statement directed at and to Scrooge as they observe the Christmas party celebration staged and led by Old Fezziwig, we see and feel the elements of true repentance taking hold within Ebenezer Scrooge:

**"A small matter," said the Ghost, "to make these silly folks so full of gratitude."

"Small!" echoed Scrooge.

The Spirit signed to him to listen to the two apprentices, who were pouring out their hearts in praise of Fezziwig: and when he had done so, said, "Why! Is it not? He has spent but a few pounds of your mortal money: three or four, perhaps. Is that so much that he deserves this praise?"

"It isn't that," said Scrooge, heated by the remark, and speaking unconsciously like his former, not his latter, self. "It isn't that, Spirit. He has the power to render us happy or unhappy; to make our service light or burdensome; a pleasure or a toil. Say that his power lies in words and looks; in things so slight and insignificant that it is impossible to add and count 'em up: what then? The happiness he gives, is quite as great as if it cost a fortune."

Scrooge then continues to speak, and while doing so, he laments to the Spirit that he would like to have a word with his own employee. Here, Scrooge begins to see, understand, and repent. This is pure writing genius.

It is important to understand that Scrooge repents early in the story and not at the end. Even when he hangs his head and **"Was overcome with penitence and grief" when the Ghost of Christmas Present tells of the future fate of Tiny Tim; this is simply a reinforcement of his earlier repentance.

Dickens establishes the fact that Scrooge repents early in the story. First off, his repentance to his former evil ways and behavior is clear in the conversation when Scrooge sees his former lonely self at his school, while left alone for Christmas. Hence, forth, Scrooge speaks to the Ghost of Christmas Past about how he wishes that he gave the Christmas carolers who all stopped by his place of business some coins for their efforts. Then later, in Stave Two (the use of staves instead of chapter markers is another brilliant reference to the carol), we have the aforementioned conversation and observations at Mr. Fezziwig's Christmas party.

Truly, the readers need to not lose sight of these two elements of repentance; one provides the title of the actual story, hence, Dickens recognized the importance of the incident and, next, the resulting observation of Old Fezziwig at his party, provided the change in attitude towards his own employee. What happens in later visits of the later Ghosts establishes the new direction that Scrooge will take in what remains of his life.

Often when I discuss this book with various interested and somewhat uninterested companions, inevitably, a person asks me if I feel as if Scrooge imagines the various Ghosts and the Ghost of old Jacob Marley within a haze of dreams, or are they real?

Great question. Let me steal a word from Mr. Dickens and use it here. A *ponderous* question! Indeed.

I feel as if they are real and Dickens felt they needed to be actual Ghostly visits by spirits to "shock" the utterly evil Ebenezer Scrooge into repentance. Deep down, God in Heaven and the powers of repentance, realized that life and circumstances brought the evil and hardness to Scrooge's heart and soul, but that he could do, and would do, goodwill towards the world and that he was worth saving. I form this opinion from digesting the author's own words in his Prelude, where he clearly references Ghosts, haunting, and even calls his work **"A Ghostly little book." The capital letters utilized by Mr. Dickens are on purpose. A further clue as to his use of proper nouns in the reference. Pure genius exposed once more.

Mr. Dickens wrote *A Christmas Carol* when he was in a dire financial situation and despite selling out on the first few days of sales and printings, it initially did not bring Mr. Dickens much financial gain. This was because of the cost of printing the book and illustrations. Of course, later, it brought fame and some baubles and coins to Mr. Dickens. I wonder if when he wrote it, if he realized the power and magnitude that the book would have in the world. I think not, but I must think that Mr. Dickens knew that he wrote an exceptional book! Authors can feel when a composition is exceptional.

Dickens's masterpiece gave birth to some of the fictional world's greatest and most memorable characters. Movies, screenplays, theater, the arts, cartoons, adaptive books, and work, in fact, every depiction that one can ever think of all resulted from approximately 28,000 or thereabouts in a word count mixed in with pure unadulterated genius. A short book, a novella, but every word and sentence contain great power and is strategic in use.

Even today, we label grumpy folks as "Scrooges" and poor folks as "Cratchits."

By the way, Mr. Magoo made a helluva Scrooge.

Some say that Mr. Dickens invented Christmas as it exists today, and from this author in this commentary, you will find a complete agreement with that statement. I believe it is a fact.

I do not want to wander into too much supposition here, but it is my hope that Mr. Charles Dickens wrote *A Christmas Carol* with an open spirit of sharing his words and genius with the world to help make it a better place, to enhance Christmas, and to open the eyes and hearts of cold-hearted people. I am not naïve in this aspect of the work and our profession. Christmas, as a subject, invokes powerful emotions.

Powerful emotions tend to sell books rather easily.

Dickens loved Christmas and used that love to his advantage, and while he wrote several Christmas stories, and some of them are quality works, none of them ever reached the majesty of *A Christmas Carol*. Yet, I hope that he endeavored not only to write the story solely for financial gain.

My work has brought me little money, if any, but that is not why I write. I write to share parts and pieces of my heart and soul within the pages of my books and to contribute to the world of books and readers. It takes great courage to do so. This world is full of mean-spirited critics, and there are many of them. If my words bring me a few coins and some dollars, then that is wonderful. If not, perhaps, I echo the words of Scrooge's nephew when he speaks of Christmas and says, **"Despite the fact that it never put a scrap of gold or silver in my pocket, I believe that it has done me good, and will do me good; and I say, God bless it!"

I read *A Christmas Carol* every Christmas season, usually, on Christmas Eve, as does my character of Chadwick Ripplewood Junior in my Christmas Book, *Ye Olde Book Shoppe*. It is a tradition, and I stole the tradition and used it in my book for my character to enjoy.

After a close examination of my intent, perhaps, it is in a subliminal effort to inspire readers to adopt the tradition and do the same.

Regardless, every reading of the story brings something new to light that I missed previously.

It is that magnificent.

A Christmas Carol endures forever, not because it is a story of one man's repentance from evil to good, or it displays the true meaning of Christmas. It endures because it conveys no matter how dark our world is, or how corrupt it is, or how cynical, that underneath the dirty side of life, goodness and love always exists. This is a story of hope and of joy, and of how, despite the circumstances of the weary world, and I am quite sure the world was weary in the world of Mr. Dickens, just as it is now, that hope and joy triumphs. Those facts, alone and forever, make this the greatest story ever written. Please, dear reader, if you take this as a story that simply exemplifies the true meaning of Christmas, then you miss the depth of the story. Please look past that and feel the depth of the story.

Enjoy it, hold it, absorb it, hold the story's message and meaning near and dear to your heart, and I assure you that you will not regret it.

Moreover, dear reader, please, I wish you a very happy Christmas. Not just right now, or this Christmas, or the next Christmas, but now, and forever more.

Mr. Paul John Hausleben

27 December 2020

** Quotes are from various books and versions of *A Christmas Carol* by Mr. Charles Dickens. This work is public domain work and used within this commentary to promote the brilliance and significance of the work in literary history.

Paul John Hausleben

Here we go with some fun with PJH lists of various Christmas-related items. Solely, my opinions, of course. I am sure you have your own favorites or clunkers.

Here are mine.

(Reminder on the order of the lists: Number five is great. Number one is superlative. With some lists, number five is not too swift and number one is simply awful).

• • • •

<u>My Top Video Versions of A Christmas Carol</u>
5. Mr. Magoo's Christmas Carol. (cartoon/musical) Tied with A Muppets Christmas Carol.
4. A Christmas Carol starring Mr. George C. Scott.
3. An American Christmas Carol starring Mr. Henry Winkler.
2. Scrooge starring Mr. Alastair Sim.
1. Scrooge starring Mr. Albert Finney. (a musical version. Mr. Finney won a Golden Globe Award for his performance. He should have won an Oscar too)

• • • •

<u>My Top Five Characters from A Christmas Carol</u>
5. Fred, Scrooge's Nephew.
4. The Ghost of Christmas Present.
3. Bob Cratchit.
2. Ebenezer Scrooge.
1. Old Fezziwig.

<u>My Top Christmas Albums from the "Golden Age of Christmas Music Recordings"</u>
5. The Spirit of Christmas with The Living Strings.
4. Christmas Favorites by The Hollyridge Strings.
3. Christmas Carols, Montavani.
2. Hallelujah (re-released as Music of Christmas, Volume 2) Percy Faith and his Orchestra.
1. Music of Christmas, Percy Faith, and his Orchestra.

• • • •

<u>My Top Christmas Albums from the "Modern Age of Christmas Music Recordings"</u>
5. The Twelve Tales of Christmas, Tom Chaplin.
4. Let It Be Christmas, Alan Jackson.
3. Christmas in The Heart, Bob Dylan.
2. Every day is Christmas, Sia.
1. The Jethro Tull Christmas Album, Jethro Tull.

• • • •

<u>My Choices for The Five Most Annoying Christmas Songs</u>
5. I Want a Hippopotamus for Christmas.
4. I'm Gettin' Nuttin' for Christmas.
3. All I Want for Christmas is My Two Front Teeth.
2. The Chipmunk Song and it is a tie with Dominic the Donkey. (oh, those awful he-haws)
1. The Twelve Days of Christmas. (how I wish there were only four days in this song)

<u>My Choices for The Five Christmas Songs That I Always Turn Off</u>
5. Santa Claus is Coming to Town, Bruce Springsteen version. (Sorry, Bruce, I still want to grab a beer with you someday)

4. Christmas Shoes (silly, slobbery, drivel)

3. All I Want for Christmas is You (please just go away!)

2. Grandma Got Run Over by a Reindeer. (really?)

1. Last Christmas. (and I promise to turn this song off every Christmas after that one too)

• • • •

<u>My Choices for The Five Dumbest Christmas Items</u>

5. Reindeer antlers and a red nose for placing upon your vehicle.

4. Blow-up, air-balloon display thingies (especially the Ferris wheel) for displaying outside of your house (almost every single one of them deflates or blows over and tilt on their sides. Nothing says Happy Christmas quite as weirdly as these blow-up air-balloon thingies)

3. Santa Claus hat, beard, and suit that installs on your toilet bowl cover and seat.

2. Christmas-themed toilet tissue.

1. Elf slippers or shoes with curled up toes and jingle bells on the ends.

<u>The Five Items That I Must Have Every Christmas</u>

5. Pine Incense.

4. Christmas tree scented candle.

3. Chocolate-covered cherries.

2. A tin of Danish butter cookies.

1. A new selection of Christmas music.

• • • •

<u>My Top Five Best Recordings of Christmas Songs</u>

5. It Must Be Santa, Bob Dylan's Version (don't miss the video)

4. Jingo-Jango, Bert Kaempfert (don't miss the light-show video on this one)

3. Santa's Got a Brand-new Bag, The Hollyridge Strings.

2. Deck the Halls, Percy Faith, and his Orchestra.

1. Joy to the World, Percy Faith, and his Orchestra.

••••

<u>The Five Things That I Do Every Christmas Day</u>
5. Listen to Her Majesty, (now, His Majesty) The King/Queen's Christmas message.
4. Listen to Christmas music.
3. Eat turkey, drink beer, and sample some special Irish or Scotch whiskey and whisky.
2. Turn all the lights out in the house and then sit, think, and stare at the Christmas tree.
1. Pray for a better world.

••••

<u>The Five Things That I Do Every Boxing Day</u>
5. Set up a holiday party table with a small Christmas tree decorated with lights and assorted beer bottle caps as ornaments, food, drink, special glassware, and a fancy tablecloth.
4. Listen to Premier League football matches. Go Nottingham Forest!
3. Eat leftover turkey, drink beer, and sample some special Irish or Scotch whiskey and whisky.
2. Listen to Christmas music.
1. Cook with steam, then light up a Christmas pudding with flaming rum and after not burning the house down, eat and enjoy it.

••••

<u>My Choices for The Five Sure-Fire Gifts That No One Ever Returns</u>
5. Gift cards.
4. Gift cards.
3. Gift cards.

2. Gift cards.
1. Love.

. . . .

About Mr. Charles Dickens

Critics, experts, and readers all consider and agree that Mr. Charles Dickens is one of the greatest authors in history. Modern or otherwise. His legendary work includes hundreds of short stories and notes as well as famous novels such as *Oliver Twist, David Copperfield, Bleak House, A Tale of Two Cities,* and of course, the famous novella, *A Christmas Carol.*

Charles Dickens was born in 1812 near Portsmouth, England, where his father was a clerk in the navy pay office. The family moved to London in 1823, but it severely impaired their fortunes. The family sent Mr. Dickens as a youngster to work in a blacking-warehouse when the courts imprisoned his father for debt. Both experiences deeply affected the future novelist. It is obvious from his work that his difficult and painful life experiences dwelled inside of his heart and manifested in his words and in his characters. In 1833, he began contributing stories to newspapers and magazines, and in 1836 started the serial publication of *Pickwick Papers.* Thereafter, Mr. Dickens published his major novels over the course of the next twenty years, from *Nicholas Nickleby* to *Little Dorrit.* He also edited the journals *Household Words* and *All the Year Round.*

Mr. Dickens died in June 1870. His multitude of colorful characters and his writings endure forever.

About
Mr. Paul John Hausleben

• • • •

• • • •

WAY BACK IN TIME, WHEN the dinosaurs first died off, at the ripe old age of sixteen, Paul John Hausleben, wrote three stories for a creative writing class in high school. Enrolled in a vocational school, and immersed in trade courses and apprenticeship, left little time for writing ventures, but PJH wrote three exceptional and entertaining stories. Paul John Hausleben's stories caught the eye of two English teachers in the college-preparatory academic programs, and they pulled the author out of his basic courses and plopped him in advanced English and writing courses. One of the English teachers had immense faith in Paul's talents, and she took PJH's stories, helped him brush them up, and submitted them to a periodical for publication. To PJH's astonishment, the periodical published all three of the stories and sent him a royalty check for fifty dollars and . . . that was it. PJH did not write anymore because life got in his way. Fast forward to 2009 and while living on the road in Atlanta, Georgia (and struggling to communicate with the locals who did not speak New Jersey) for his full-time job, PJH took a part-time job writing music reviews for a progressive rock website, and that gig caused the writing bug to bite PJH once more. He recalled those old stories and found the old manuscripts hiding in

121

a dusty box. After some doodling around with them, PJH decided to revisit them. Two stories became the nucleus for the anthology now known as, *The Time Bomb in The Cupboard and Other Adventures of Harry and Paul.* The other story became the anchor story for collection known as, *The Christmas Tree and Other Christmas Stories, Tales for a Christmas Evening.* Now, many years and over thirty-five published works later, along with countless blogs and other work, PJH continues to write. Where and when it stops, only the author really knows.

On the other hand, does he really know?

If you ask Paul John Hausleben, he will tell you that he is not an author, he is just a storyteller. His mission is to continue to write and tell stories to warm your heart, make you laugh, and sometimes make you cry, just a little. Most of all, he deals in memories, and helps you to remember the good times of your own life, and the special people who touched you along the way. Paul was born and raised in Paterson, and then nearby Haledon, New Jersey, and began writing at an early age. He revisited a writing career later in his life, and he now is the author of several novels, compilations, short stories and audio and video works. Most of his work touches upon nostalgic remembrances of simpler times, and tells the stories of heartfelt, humorous, and special human relationships. Other than writing, among many careers both paid and unpaid, he is a former semi-professional hockey goaltender, a music fan and music reviewer, an avid sports fan, photographer, and amateur radio operator. He now resides in Somewhere, U.S.A., but his heart always remains along Belmont Avenue in good old Paterson, and Haledon, New Jersey.

Other Work by Mr. Paul John Hausleben

The Time Bomb in The Cupboard and Other Adventures of Harry and Paul
The Night Always Comes, Another story from the Adventures of Harry and
Paul
Reunion, A sequel to the Night Always Comes and Another story from the
Adventures of Harry and Paul
The Miracle Tree, Another story from the Adventures of Harry and Paul
The Chronicles of Henson
Heaven's Gain
The Final Adventure of Harry and Paul
Geyer Street Gardens
Beneath the Mask of a Hockey Goaltender
Another story from the Adventures of Harry and Paul
Where the River Bends and Curls
Tales of the Quiet Stranger in the Black Hat
Crows on a High Wire
Reflections, The Christmas Collection
The Christmas Tree and Other Christmas Stories,
Tales for a Christmas Evening
Christmas Cocktails
The Many Cases of Detective Lyle Odell
Experiences. A Series of Essays on My Life
And a few others too!

You may write to the author at the email address of ctte27@gmail.com

Published by God Bless the Keg Publishing LLC
Henrico, Virginia, U.S.A.
You may write to the publisher at Godblessthekegpublishing@gmail.com

"Life's simple pleasures are so often the best ones!"
Follow Paul John Hausleben and God Bless the Keg Publishing LLC on
Facebook and enjoy samples of his photography, receive updates on new
releases, and enjoy his general meanderings

Don't miss out!

Visit the website below and you can sign up to receive emails whenever Paul John Hausleben publishes a new book. There's no charge and no obligation.

https://books2read.com/r/B-A-SOFC-EOGZE

BOOKS 2 READ

Connecting independent readers to independent writers.